TERRI BRISBIN

BOOK 45

The Ghosts of Culloden Moor
A Scottish Paranormal Romance

Published by Luckenbooth Press.

ISBN: 978-0-9996540-9-5

Book Cover Design: © Kelli Ann Morgan of
Inspire Creative Services

Formatting: Nina Pierce of Seaside Publications

THE STORYTELLER

TERRI BRISBIN

Prologue

Struan Cameron looked out on Drummossie Moor and saw nothing but the mist swirling before him. Only with great effort could he begin to pick out the others there in the thick, white fog. He let out a breath that did not move the mist around him. He had not had an effect on the world since that day, the sixteenth of April in the year of our Lord seventeen hundred and forty-six. The day he fell in battle. The day he and the others here died.

They were fewer now than that day or the next when the seventy-nine spirits rose on the battlefield. Soncerae, the young but powerful Muir witch, had begun calling them to her and sending them off … somewhere. None had returned and Struan wondered when his time would come and how she chose those she summoned.

Mayhap he should fear her, fear her power, fear whatever was to come? Oh, aye, she'd tried to explain it to them before she began, but he knew not yet if he would seek his vengeance on the Bonnie Prince as she'd offered or not. Struan did not doubt that God Almighty would forgive them if they sought to punish the man for the willful destruction his actions and desires had brought to Scotland and the clans here in the Highlands. Facing their final judgment now, more than two hundred and fifty years after their deaths, made him consider what his choice would be.

As he watched one and then another approach the lass and disappear, he knew it was a different sort of thing from the way he could fade away. That happened sometimes when, after telling his stories to the others, he lost the ability or strength to stay here on this field of tremendous loss and injustice and he would just let go. 'Twas never for long. 'Twas never completely in his control. One moment he was there and the next … well, he was not.

After some time, Struan would wake or come to awareness in the same position and place where he'd died, in the middle of the moor where the fighting had been the worst. His right arm, his sword arm, sliced off by an English soldier, lay separated from his body on the ground next to him. The only good thing was that just as this form in which he existed lacked form and substance, it also lacked the ability to feel pain.

Now, the mist scattered as young Soni walked over the moor toward him. Struan stood to meet her and watched as her expression softened. She reached out to him, her cloak flowing around her slight body. The bright green ring of power that surrounded her ebbed and flowed with each step she took.

"Struan Cameron, 'tis yer turn," she said softly. "If ye succeed, the choice will be yers."

A nervousness he'd not felt in centuries filled him as he rose to his full height and nodded. A tension tugged on him, pulling him closer to the lass.

"Ye have up to two days, Struan," she said softly. "Two days to prove ye are worthy for the reward awaiting ye."

Struan frowned at her. "Reward? I just want an end to this," he said. He swept his arm out to point across the moor. "All of this." The endless suffering of those souls trapped here—neither truly dead and not alive.

"And ye shall have that and a chance to face the man responsible for this, if ye are worthy." She lifted her hand and motioned toward the moor. Then, she turned her gaze back to him. "Are ye ready then, Storyteller?" Soni reached out her hand to touch his. He'd watched her touch some of the others before, but only the one called seventy-nine had seemed to feel it. Struan had never himself.

"Do ye ken where I go?" he asked. His voice was nothing more than a whisper across the eerie silence that settled over the moor.

"Aye, Struan, I do." The lass smiled then and he felt the fear drift away. "Just remember to tell yer stories and I think all will be well."

"My stories?"

Struan passed the time—the endless days and nights spent here since the fateful battle, now called Culloden—telling stories he'd heard while growing up in his village and stories of glorious battles and even of the days leading up to the one that killed him. He even told the tale of that day which, he kenned now, would end the kind of life they'd all known here in the Highlands of Scotland. The stories he told, however, did not usually end in that tragic and true way.

"Aye, Storyteller," Soni said with a nod. "Someone needs to hear yer story now."

He puzzled on her words only moments before she reached out across those final inches to him. He could not feel her touch, but something, some kind of sensation, traveled through the form he held.

Then, without warning, everything and everyone around him disappeared and he only knew he was no longer on Drummossie Moor.

Chapter One

November, 2015
Southern Coast of Maine, near Serenity Harbor

The tears fell unbidden but not unexpectedly. Fiona Masters did not brush them away as she glanced around the living room of the large cabin once more. Her life had been lived here, with her family and friends, and so it seemed somehow right that it should end here, too.

Photos of her family spread around the room reminded her of those happy times. Times she had no idea would end when or how they did. Times when she believed in happily-ever-after. Times when she thought she would have years or decades with those she loved.

Pulling in a ragged breath and letting it go, Fee memorized the smiles and the faces of her parents, her sister and brother, her ex-fiancé even, before turning and walking out. The crispness of the cool autumn morning here on the coast of Maine was a balm to her soul, but it was too little and much, much too late.

The tightness that stiffened the muscles in her leg reminded her with every step away she took.

The thick scars that still painfully crisscrossed her hand as she clutched the walking stick reminded her. The way she tucked her head down and away as she walked was another. Scarred, empty and weary of struggling, Fee had returned here to end her life and end the pain and shame and suffering of the last three years.

Fee followed the steep path up to the cliffside, having a care to take her time and watch her steps. The three years of physical therapy had not restored the strength and agility damaged by the injuries to her leg. Fee touched her coat and felt the outline of the gun there.

It had taken weeks of practice to learn to control the gun with her right hand. The scar tissue and damage to the muscles in her left, her dominant hand, made it impossible to curl her fingers around the trigger. So, after depending on her left hand all her life, Fee would have to take this final action using her right one.

After what seemed a long time, she struggled across the final paces to the edge of the ocean. The Atlantic was in fine form this morning, tossing waves against the impervious Maine coast where it met the bay. Finally reaching the top, Fee eased her way to the very edge and stood there, staring out at the relentless ocean.

Not long ago, standing here like this would have refreshed and energized her. It had been her habit to watch the movement of the water, to try to count the countless whitecaps as the winds pushed the water to batter the rocks below. Now though, even after several minutes of staring out across to the eastern horizon, the emptiness in her did not fill.

Fee understood that that emotional void would never be full. Too much loss, too much tragedy and too much damage had emptied her and left her unable to face a life such as it was. She slipped her hand inside that pocket again and touched the gun that would see her out of physical pain forever. Pain was a good thing, her counselor had told her. It spoke of something other than relentless emptiness and that, the counselor assured her, meant she could heal.

Well, that counselor was wrong.

Fee glanced below to the rocks at the base of the cliff. Those were her 'plan b' if for some reason the gun didn't work or her aim was off. Flinging the walking stick on which she depended away, she slid her fingers around the gun and pulled it from her pocket. It was loaded—she'd done that before leaving her parents' cabin—so all she needed to do was place it against her and pull that trigger.

Lifting it to her head, Fee cocked the trigger and touched the short barrel to the base of her neck. Then, remembering what she'd read, she moved it under her jaw, aiming it differently. Expecting to feel fear or trepidation or doubt, yet all she felt was … nothing. Balancing with the sun and wind and sea at her back, Fee closed her eyes and swallowed, tightening her finger on the trigger.

"Are ye daft, lass?" A loud, furious voice stopped her finger and made her open her eyes. A large man strode toward her, his long strides covering the ground at an amazing pace. "Give that over now!" he yelled.

Surprised by his arrival, his size and his speed, Fee pulled the trigger of the Ruger. Unfortunately for her, the continued shouting in some foreign language and the sight of him startled her and her aim was off. Unfortunately for him, she shot him in the arm. She wobbled at the edge of the cliff, watching as he barely slowed in his approach.

The blooming red on the sleeve of his shirt drew her attention then. She'd always had a problem with the sight of blood and this growing stain triggered that automatic reaction in her. Her stomach churned and acid flushed up into her mouth. Her body reacted before her mind could fully understand the situation and Fiona fell into the blackness.

A blackness she hoped would be the end of things.

Struan did not allow the shock and pain to slow him. The lass who'd shot him now tumbled down in a faint and, in another moment, she would pitch headlong over the cliffside on which she stood. As her eyes fluttered up and closed, he ran, crossing the final yards to her, and grabbed hold of her coat. The gun in her hand clattered on the rocks at her feet as he scooped her up into his arms and carried her away from the edge. Laying her on a grassy patch of ground, he took his first true look at the lass.

The rise and fall of her chest told him she lived and breathed—a good sign that. Though there were scars on her hands that spoke of previous injuries, there were no marks of more recent ones. Content that she would wake soon, Struan stood and grabbed his arm. His burning, pain-filled arm.

Strange, for the arm she'd shot had been gone for over two hundred years. Slashed off by an enemy's sword during the battle, it had been the cause of his death. Now, it was there—flesh and blood once more. From the throbbing and bleeding, he guessed the ball had gone through or simply grazed him. Tearing off the sleeve, he found a flesh wound and used the fabric to dab at the blood.

A moan from the lass brought him back to her side. Kneeling there, he slid his hand under her head to lift it when the hood she wore fell back, revealing her face to him. A web of scars covered her brow, her cheeks and down onto her jaw and neck. The thickened skin pulled on her eye, narrowing it. Only her mouth had been spared from whatever terrible injury had caused the rest.

As he gazed at her perfect mouth, Struan could not ever remember seeing a lass with such injuries, though he'd seen many, many men with such wounds after battles and fights. The explosions of the cannons during Culloden would cause such damage as this and more.

Her eyes fluttered then and he watched as she came back to herself and saw him. The color of them reminded him of the brilliant blue of the sky over him when he'd died that day so long ago. The instant she was aware of herself, she struggled to her knees and scuttled away, glancing around the area until her gaze fell on the weapon she'd held.

It struck him in that moment.

Her purpose.

The reason she'd stood there on the cliff with a gun in her hand. He'd blessed himself before he could stop it. She met his gaze and turned away then, tears streaming down her cheeks in silence.

Suicide.

She'd meant to end her life.

Struan understood too well the hopelessness of grief and pain to belittle or question her choice. In the years leading up to and after Culloden, he and each of the seventy-nine had struggled with it in some way. Having the knowledge of what had happened after that battle and watching the decades and centuries pass without their loved ones or the ability to pass on from their ghostly existence kindled the hard edge of desperation in their souls. If he was being honest, his stories had been a way to battle that darkness that sought to snuff out every bit of them that still existed. Still … The heart now beating in his chest hurt for her as she'd faced such a dire decision as that one.

"What is yer name, lass?" he asked softly. Struan stood then and backed away a pace. At first her gaze remained on the gun, but he spoke again, finally gaining her attention. "What are ye called?"

"Fiona … Fee," she stuttered out. "My name is Fiona."

Struan took the few steps needed to reach her and held out his hand to her. "Struan Cameron, at yer service."

He'd used his right arm, the one that yet bled and he watched the scant bit of color in her face flee once more. Clearly the lass had no tolerance of blood. Turning away, he tore off his other sleeve and used it to quickly bandage his injury, wrapping it tightly to stanch the bleeding. When he turned back to her, he was surprised to find her standing.

"I did not mean to hurt you," she said, nodding at his injury. "The gun … it misfired … my bad hand …" The shadows in her eyes as she tucked her hand against her side to hide it bothered him. She was shamed by her actions and shamed, it seemed, by her appearance. And now, she sought to explain the terrible truth.

"No bother, lass," he said, shrugging and shaking his head at her. "I have been shot afore." He shrugged again. "Several times." Struan glanced down at his arm, the one that now throbbed in pain for the first time in more than two hundred years, and he smiled. "I didna expect it to sting so much." He laughed then, feeling the very air as his chest expanded drawing in deep breaths. "I didna expect to feel any of this again." Her brows gathered into a frown and he shook his head. "No bother."

"There are supplies at the cabin," she said, looking off in the distance behind him. "It should be cleaned at least." She gagged as she said the words, making it very clear that she would not be the one seeing to it.

He scooped up the gun and held it, waiting for her to lead the way. Her hesitation made him understand that she meant him to go on without her. Did she mean to finish the deed then? Struan stepped aside and gave her the choice, but in his mind, it had to be a choice. He raised the hand holding the weapon out a bit, so she could take it if she so desired. He did not meet her gaze, giving her a chance to examine her own thoughts in that moment.

He could not help but smile when she instead moved in front of him and led the way into the trees and down a path there without taking the gun from him. When she peeked over her shoulder to see if he followed, he tucked the gun in his belt, nodded at her and walked a pace behind her.

"My grandmam shot all three of her husbands, ye ken," he began. When she stopped and looked on him in horror, he continued the tale as they walked. "She had her reasons. Good ones, too, if ye ask me. The first one was a mean bastard …"

Chapter Two

She'd lost her mind. That was the only explanation for this. Oh, when the decision to kill herself entered her thoughts, Fee had feared for her sanity, but she'd never doubted that she understood her actions. Now? Well, she had to question herself thoroughly.

As they walked slowly down the path back to the cabin, Struan Cameron spoke. His deep voice with that sexy Scottish accent was so easy to listen to, so she did. His story about his grandmother and her longstanding habit of shooting the men in her life was humorous and too funny to be true, but Fee appreciated the way he filled the uncomfortable silence.

And she was grateful for the way, at some point in

the walk, he'd held out his arm and she steadied herself using his strength. Too late, she remembered tossing the walking stick she used away. When she stumbled for the third time, he let out a loud sigh and scooped her up in his arms. She thought about arguing with him, that she could make it on her own, but he simply continued speaking about his grandmother and really didn't give her the opportunity to say a word.

When he'd appeared in that last moment, she thought she'd conjured him up somehow. He wore a Scottish kilt, for gosh sakes, and looked as if he'd stepped off a reenactment field or out of a TV show. The muscles in the strong arms that held her were real. The heartbeat that pulsed against her arm was real. Worse though, the blood pouring from his arm after she'd shot him was hard to ignore, too.

Damn it, she could not stand the sight of it! When she'd come to and he'd stood over her staring down, she'd felt his strong hand holding her head off the ground. She'd looked into eyes as dark green as the leaves on the trees around them. Though she expected to see censure or anger there, instead she found empathy and sadness.

Even when he realized what she'd been planning—and she'd noticed the change in his gaze the moment he did—she never saw pity or disgust. What a strange, strange man. What a strange, surreal situation. And yet, his "normal" actions of introducing himself and ignoring the fact that she'd shot him somehow put her at ease.

As though waking from sleep, Fee found herself lost in her confused thoughts and feelings and unable to focus then. She'd expected to die. She'd expected to never have to interact with others again. And now, minutes after she'd placed the gun and touched her finger to the trigger, she faced someone without understanding who he was or how he'd come to be there on the cliffside.

Fee reached out and pushed some branches out of their way until he reached to grab them. The heat pouring off him surrounded her then and, for a moment, she wanted him to wrap her arms around him. She ached for a true embrace, even of a stranger. Just a moment of compassion. Caring. Tears burned her eyes and she cursed herself for the fool she was. His arrival would only be a delay in her plan. Once she'd let him clean up, he would leave and she would … end things.

He was still telling his story when they walked into the clearing that held her parents' cabin. There was something in the way he spoke that convinced her he was definitely not a local. Serenity Harbor across the bay drew visitors from all over the world and, had it been the season, she would have no doubt that he was heading or visiting there. But the tourist season was over now and that left only the townies to inhabit the island and surrounding villages and campgrounds.

Fee admitted to herself she'd not paid much attention to any announcements or mailings from the administrators of the nearby camp about reenactments or shows on the grounds. Even so, it was possible that there was a simple explanation for his appearance. He carried her up to the front door and once she regained her balance, she stepped closer to it and reached up to get the key.

"Here, let me," he said.

His height made it an easy thing and he slid his hand along the ledge of the door until he found the key. Handing it to her, he stepped back. She unlocked and opened the door, walking back into one place she never expected to be again. The photos still sat there, but now they seemed to mock her failure. It was her own guilt and sense of failure, Fee knew that, but she looked away and to the man who was now silent behind her.

"The bathroom is through there," she said, pointing down the hallway that led to the two bedrooms and bathroom on this floor. "I'll get the first aid kit for you."

Fee walked into the kitchen area on unsteady legs and opened the cabinet closest to the back door. All the necessities were stored there—first aid kit, flashlights, batteries, emergency radio and more. Only when she'd gathered up what she thought he needed and stood did she realized he'd not moved.

"Are you all right?" she asked, walking back to him. It was easier to get around on smooth, flat surfaces. Taking in his height and build, she knew for sure that, if he fell or collapsed, there was no way possible for her to hold him up or get him back on his feet. "If you'd rather use this sink, it might be easier?" She nodded at the deep, double-wide sink there under the windows. Her mother's pride-and-joy when they'd renovated and expanded the cabin four years ago. "There are towels in that drawer."

Fee laid out the disinfectant soap, the antibiotic cream, the bandages and tape and stepped away. Struan slid his fingers into the handle and eased the drawer open in an almost child-like way of doing something for the first time. He slid it closed and then opened it once more. And then again. His strange behavior made her think he was the woozy one here.

"If you faint, I won't be able to save you," she admitted aloud to him.

He snorted and let out a harsh breath before opening the drawer and grabbing a stack of the folded towels. She would have moved away to give him some room to see to his injury but he just stared now at the sink and the faucet and spigots as though he'd never seen anything like it.

Her mother's tastes usually ran to the traditional, but she went all-out new and futuristic when she redid this kitchen. The faucet was a multi-purpose wonder that included sensors, a spigot that could be a hose and even automatic temperature controls. Mary Richards might be a country girl at heart, but she wanted her kitchen to be the height of urban design.

"You wave your hand here to turn it on. Swipe your finger this way for warmer," she demonstrated as she spoke, "and this way for cooler." She pushed the button to release the built-in hose. "And use this if it's too hard to maneuver your shoulder and arm under there."

Fee stepped back and watched as he began to experiment with all the settings and pieces. Like he had with the drawer, Struan acted as though he'd never turned on a faucet and he continued to turn it on and off, changing the settings and the force and the temperature of it until he seemed to grasp all of it.

"'Tis a fine thing, Fiona," he called out to her. Since she knew he'd have to open the rough bandage he'd made and there would be bleeding, Fee made her way over to the living room area and sunk into one of the overstuffed chairs there. "I have never seen the like."

"Where are you from?" she asked.

"Scotland," he answered in a prideful tone. "Where is this place?" His accent thick, it made some words hard to understand at first, so she answered the question she thought he'd asked.

"My parents' cabin."

"I thought as much," he said. Struan turned off the water and walked closer. "Where does it sit?" She frowned. "Where are we?"

There was so much he did not know and could not understand in this place. So much he wanted to know and to ask her about. Oh, he and the others had watched the years pass and had witnessed many, many changes. In clothing. In roads and transportation. In buildings and such. In the way people lived and the way they acted. The lands around Drummossie Moor had changed over the decades and centuries and the seventy-nine had watched it all.

When he appeared before her, Struan knew he was not in Highlands or even in Scotland. As he looked around at the cliffs and the large bay, it felt very close to the places where he'd lived and grown but he knew it to be a faraway land. Her voice told him she was an American. So, he knew that's where he was. From her garb, it was the same time and same season of year as when Soni had summoned him. But where exactly was he?

"I have been traveling for some time and am … all turned about in my directions," he offered. Her features eased and she nodded.

"We are to the south and west of Serenity Harbor," she said. "Maine." She pointed back toward the cliff where he'd found her. "I thought you might be heading there? It's a huge tourist destination."

"Ah, Serenity Harbor," he said. It sounded like a grand place, but Struan had never heard it or Maine either. "Maine," he said with a nod. "I am from a small town in Scotland. These modern conveniences have not made it to my town yet."

He tried to remember the words and phrases he'd heard from visitors to the battlefield. These must have worked for her worried expression eased as she leaned back in the chair as he spoke.

"Tell me of your small town."

As he considered how and what to tell her, he noticed that she seemed to be swallowed up by that chair. Another quick glance revealed the exhaustion that dulled her gaze and made her look drawn and pale now.

How she had walked herself up that hillside to the edge, he knew not. He'd bided his time, recognizing that she would never make it down the path on her own. When she began to stumble, her legs not holding steady, he lifted her slight form and carried her the rest of the way here.

Struan looked over the items she'd gathered and began to speak about his village and its location not far from Achnacarry, near Lochs Arkaig and Lochy. The words about his family did not come easily to him so he told her more about his chieftain who had called him to fight for the rights of the dispossessed king across the water. He spoke of their lands and extended kin. But he chose not to speak of his closest kin, for it pained him too much.

"My village is a smattering of cottages and tradesmen gathered where the River Arkaig empties into Loch Lochy," he said softly. "My parents farmed lands there."

Whether shock was setting in now or exhaustion overwhelming her, he could not decipher. Her eyes fluttered a few times and then closed as he talked.

Struan continued speaking of this and that until her breathing eased and evened into sleep. Then, his interest piqued, he walked back to the miracle of modern plumbing in the kitchen and saw to his wound. 'Twas mostly just bleeding without serious damage as he'd thought. He unwrapped his plaid, rinsed out the bloodied spots and laid it over a chair to dry. But touching his arm, the one that had been hacked off in battle, sent shivers through him. He was whole once more. He was, taking in a deep breath and exhaling it to prove it to himself, alive and breathing.

Soni was truly a powerful witch to be able to give him this time though he'd been so long dead. And to experience it in his own body, returned and renewed, was nothing short of a miracle. But, why? Why him? Why here? Why now?

Fee muttered and whispered in her sleep and he walked to her side there. Was she the reason? Was he meant to stop her from taking her own life? Or meant to witness her act? Nay, not to witness but to stop, he was certain.

Had he succeeded then, in the task Soni set for him? He looked around the room and wondered for a moment. Nay, he had not finished or surely Soni would have collected him. So, there was something more for him to do here. The lass shivered then and, for the first time in such a long time, Struan noticed the gooseflesh on his now-bared arms. Cold. He felt the cold and reveled in it. When she trembled in the chilly air once more, he knew what he needed to do.

It took a few minutes for him to make a fire in the hearth. First, he was out of practice and second, he lost some time when he found chunks of peat there among the wood. The feel of it in his hands and the smell of it filled him with a longing for home that shook him deeply. Emotions that had been muted for the last two hundred years on the moor now flared as the flames in the hearth soon did.

Struan arranged the blocks in the iron grate and lit them using one of those matches he'd seen tourists use to light cigarettes as they walked the paths of the battlefield. The earthy scent filled the room and the air grew warmer. The lass settled down deeper into the cushions and Struan brought a smaller stool to her chair. Lifting her legs as gently as he could, he positioned the stool beneath them and then tossed a blanket over her. And she slept on. Struan wandered through the cabin, marveling at so many things he saw.

The ghosts saw many things around the battlefield and when they chose to enter the visitors' center there. The 'technology' they called it—ways to see images that moved and spoke. Visitors carried 'phones' that could save images and could be used to speak to others not there. The ghosts had witnessed a great many changes while in a state that could neither impact nor participate in the flow of time that moved ever forward around them. Now though, as he moved about, Struan touched the devices and screens he found throughout the cabin and marveled over them. It mattered not to him that he had no idea of how to use those he found.

When his exploration was done, Struan returned to the living room, as she'd called it, with a book he'd found in one of the upstairs chambers. He'd not found candles to light and doubted he'd be able to read without them, but just holding a book in his hands felt good. Then, as he settled near her, something clicked and lights burst to life around him!

"Bloody hell!" He jumped up in surprise as several fixtures flashed in his face. He fell back into his Gaelic for the next words.

It was when he turned back toward the lass that he found her staring at him, her eyes wide and her mouth open. Only then did he remember removing his bloodied shirt and plaid.

Chapter Three

This must be the dream continuing, Fee thought.

She'd fallen asleep listening to his deep voice speak about … something. She remembered not wanting to let go, but the exhaustion, both physical and emotional, had taken control of her.

In the dream, she'd been whole again. No stumbling. No scars. No damage. Fee stood before the Scottish warrior and felt no shame. She'd smiled at him as he spoke in that voice that sent shivers across her skin. He took her hand and smiled back. His words became clear to her then.

His words were vows.

Vows …

Then he yelled and she startled awake. He could

curse fluently in several languages it seemed. He wore fewer clothes than when she'd closed her eyes for right now he stood before her bare-chested in only his body-hugging pants. Unable to look away from his very well-developed body, she swallowed several times, trying to bring moisture back into her mouth.

"The lights are set to go on automatically," she explained when she could force the words out. Fiona's gaze flitted over his muscular thighs, encased in pants she imagined did not allow even a molecule of air between the fabric and his skin. Heat filled her own skin. It had been a long, long time since she'd felt this way. His questioning expression and glance at the light on the end table reminded her of what had happened. "I forgot to turn the power off."

"Just so," he said with a nod.

His expression—a mix of terror, anger and confusion—belied his words of acceptance. That look was so very out of place on the face of such a big and imposing man. Yet, there it was. Again, he appeared to not know about electric lights or timed-delay controls. Even his earlier explanation of living in a small village did not explain it. The entire world knew about electric lights, even if they did not have it.

So, who was he and how had he gotten here, to the middle of nowhere, just as she was about to end her life? A crackle and pop drew her attention from him. She turned her head and glanced at the hearth.

"You made a fire." Something unfurled with her at the sight and smell of that fire, and at knowing he'd made it. She could not identify it but it made her smile. "I love the smell of the peat."

"I do as well, lass," he said. His mouth curved then and dimples settled in both of his cheeks. Rather than making him seem softer, it made him seem … more male. This Struan Cameron was a handsome man, but when he smiled, he was wickedly gorgeous. "It smells like home to me." A flash of sadness crossed his face, but was gone so quickly she doubted she'd seen it.

"How long has it been since you were there?" she asked. He did not answer her right away. Several seconds passed before he gave a sad smile and shrugged.

"A long, long time, I fear."

So much longing and sadness filled those few words that something uncurled deep within her as she watched him. A whisper of a need to comfort him. Empathy for whatever kept him from his home and those he clearly loved. Emotions she had not felt in years. Three years, two months, one week and three days, if she was counting.

"Why can you not go there? What is keeping you away?" she asked, knowing that she pried shamelessly into this stranger's life. His gaze narrowed and he let out a breath in a huff. She knew what he was about to say before he uttered another sound.

"They're all gone, lass. Every one of them."

"How? What happened?" Fee did not remember hearing of a disaster, man-made or natural, that had struck Scotland and that would explain an entire village or town being … gone?

Only when he turned in silence and walked over to the door did she realize that they had fallen into some sort of comfortable companionship that had just ended. How weird was it that she did not feel any fear of being with this complete stranger? This man could get her in a lot of trouble with just one call to the police. After all, she'd shot him. No matter that it had been an accident and he'd not been her target, questions would be raised about the gun and her use of it. More questions would follow and she would find herself unable to finish what she'd planned and started.

Now, though, her questions had brought the sense of ease with him to an end.

Fee slid back before pushing herself up to stand. Twinges in her legs told her why she should not have fallen asleep in that chair. Questions began to swirl in her mind making her realize that she was more curious about this man and his sudden appearance in front of her on the cliff than she should be. That she was *interested.*

"Struan?" she whispered. Clearing her throat, she repeated his name a little louder. "Struan." That second time, he did turn back to face her. "Would you tell me how you got here?" He frowned for a moment. Before he could speak a word, she asked another question. "Why are you here?"

Struan was sorting through his words when the funniest thing happened. A feeling he'd not had in centuries began in his belly. Well, he'd not felt the joys or weaknesses of the flesh since his death, but the one he felt now had been a constant companion during the last months of the fight against the German usurper and his ilk. His stomach rumbled loudly, bringing her lovely gaze to his body and announcing its need to both of them.

"You are hungry?" Her eyes darkened and a frown marred her brow then. "I should have … I was not thinking … Do you … ?" She stuttered through a few more beginnings before he waved her off.

"'Tis nothing to worry over, lass."

His words did not stop her from doing exactly that. Fiona walked slowly toward the area she called the kitchen and began opening the storage closets there. He'd already had a peek in them and in any he found abovestairs as well.

"I can offer you soup," she said, holding out a small item to him. It was a metal cylinder with an image of food on it. This was like no soup he'd ever seen. Then he remembered the day he had followed a tourist into the center at Culloden and watched as they purchased a meal to eat. There had been soups of all kinds, but never in small tins like this one.

"I have only the basics here now." She shrugged then. "Since the cabin isn't being used much, I didn't go grocery shopping on my way here."

Ah, she was not planning to stay here long at all then. She'd arrived and began her plan to meet death without delay. It saddened him and he did not understand why. What would drive such a woman as she to end her life? He blinked several times to clear his vision and nodded at the tin he held.

"What do I do with this, Fiona?" He held it closer and stared at the words printed all over it. *Cooking directions? Microwave?* He could read English, Gaelic and some French, but these words confused him.

"I was offering you a choice. I have the Tomato, Chicken Noodle," she began. Reaching up into the closet there, she grabbed a few more of the tins. "This one is my favorite," she said, handing it to him. *New England Clam Chowder*, it read. "They are not fancy, but they will fill you."

The image on the *Chicken Noodle* looked the most like his mother's cock-a-leekie soup so he pointed at that one. "That'll do fine."

When she glanced over her shoulder at him for the

third time, Struan stepped a pace back away from her. He made her nervous, that much was clear. And yet no matter that, she had not demanded his departure or had not tried to leave herself. His height and girth intimidated many, men and women alike. His condition—disheveled and bloodied—would give most sensible people pause. His sudden appearance and lack of knowledge about the area and times would alarm most. All those factors should have her screaming for help or calling the authorities on him. Yet she did not.

"Yer pardon for crowding ye so," he offered, giving her room to move about. "Do ye need any help?"

She asked for a thing in one of the *drawers* and by the time he understood what she meant, she had retrieved it herself. All these strange tools and bits and such confused him. Struan watched as Fiona used some gadget to grab ahold of the edge of the tin and twist it several times. He studied her hands and saw the way one did not move as smoothly as the other. Some of her fingers did not close around the gadget as others did.

He could tell that she was at ease in this place. With no lost time wasted searching for things, she opened the tin, poured the contents into a pan and placed it on the stove. A stove that needed no fire or flame to work. Fiona threw him a glance that examined him from head to toes and then she retrieved and added a second tin to the pot. She was a keen lass, understanding his hunger! Soon, far sooner as it would have taken his mother to do the same, a large bowl of steaming soup sat before him at the table there. A smaller bowl of a thicker stew awaited the lass.

When his stomach let out another loud growl, he laughed, enjoying the sensations that his body felt now. After all this time feeling nothing but the relentless passage of time, 'twas hard to believe that hunger could be a pleasure. But, he reveled in the way his belly rumbled and how his mouth watered at the delicious aroma of the soup before him.

"You haven't eaten recently?" Fiona asked as she took a sip from her spoon.

"Not in more than two hundred years, lass. Not in two hundred years."

From the way she sputtered and then choked on her spoonful of soup, mayhap honesty was not the best path after all?

Chapter Four

If he had said those words with any hint of trying to make some joke or using sarcasm, she would not have reacted that way. But there was a tone of honesty in his words that made her gasp. And the gasp made her choke on the tiny amount of soup she'd been swallowing as he'd said them. The choke turned into coughing and it took her more than a minute to finally breathe without causing the cascade of spasms again.

"Two hundred years? What do you mean by that?" If her voice was shrill or shaky, she could not help it.

Was she dealing with a lunatic? Some unfortunate who'd lost his wits and found his way to her at the very second she was finally taking action to end her misery? He seemed out-of-place to her but not crazy.

Right now, he paused before answering her, clearly deliberating on his reply. A madman did not think about what to say. The man before her was calm, made sense in most things he'd said, and acted, well, normal. With a few exceptions of course.

He *was* dressed in a Highland kilt and looked as though he'd stepped out of a reenactment. He was not familiar with any of the modern conveniences of the house. He'd not understood her directions or how to do the most basic tasks.

So …

Was he mad or was she for almost believing him now?

"Weel, Fiona Masters, it is a tale that ye might no' believe," he said softly. His voice sent its mellow tones through her and eased her in some way she could not explain. "Ye might think me a madman after I have told ye."

She thought so now. One of them was crazy. Either her for trying to end her life or him for believing he was from the past.

"Two hundred years?" she asked once more. He placed the spoon on the table, lifted the bowl and drank down the rest before speaking.

"If truth be told, closer to three hundred than two," he said with a wink. An amazing, wicked, sexy wink that distracted her for a moment.

"Nearly three hundred years then," she accepted

the words of this tale he told … for now.

"I was born on Cameron lands in the year of Our Lord seventeen hundred and twenty-three. My mam told me I came in the darkest part of the winter and the cries of the *ban-sidhe,* the woman whose cry is the harbinger of death in the Highlands, echoed down the glen." He paused then and smiled, nodding at her. "My mam thought it meant my death but instead, the keening was for my poor auntie Sarah who died that same day."

"Banshee?" Fiona had only heard the term used in slang, for someone who screeched out loudly.

"Aye, the *ban-sidhe,*" he repeated in a way she was certain she never could. His tongue rolled the words and softened the letters until it came out on a breathy tone. "Death is coming when she cries out her song of pain and loss."

"So, you were born three centuries ago? And yet you look no more than …" Fee tried not to stare at his handsome face, but she thought he could not be more than … "Twenty-five. You can't be more than twenty-five."

"I lived for three-and-twenty years before …"

"Before?" Fee held her breath then, knowing that his next words would prove one or both of them was losing their minds.

"I died on the sixteenth day in the month of April, in the year of Our Lord seventeen and forty-six."

He let out a breath when he'd spoken the words as though he expected something to happen then. He even glanced around the house, waited or looking for someone or something. But, a feeling of dread filled her as he mentioned that date.

April 16, 1746.

Anyone with any bit of Scottish blood in their veins knew that date. It was the battle that ended the Highlanders' way of life and put the clans to the sword. It was the battle of …

"Culloden." They both whispered the name together and Fee could not help but shudder at the implication of it.

He was trying to tell her he'd lived almost three centuries before and died in one of the most infamous battles in all of Scotland's history? She would have laughed then, but the dark, piercing stare that met her gaze told her that he did not joke about this.

"So, you're what? An apparition? Not really here at all?" She did laugh then, a nervous one that she was possibly imagining a man or seeing and speaking to someone who wasn't there. "All part of my imagination?"

She pushed back from the table and stumbled a bit. Her legs were always so tight after sitting still. Fee grabbed the edge of the table so tightly that her fingers lost all their color. It was hard to breathe then and she felt the panic rising inside. As he stood across from her, she backed away. Her chest tightened and her skin felt as though stretched to its limit around her body. Worse, her vision narrowed and she could see only the faintest image in front of her. Was this real? What was going on?

"Here now, lass," his voice came from much closer now. "Sit a spell and catch yer breath." His hands touched hers and the warmth of his body flowed into her. "Ye look as if ye are ready to keel over. Dinna fash, we will sort this out."

She grabbed his hands then and let him guide her back onto the chair. He knelt at her side, not pulling away, and Fee finally looked at him. Closely. He was flesh-and-blood. He'd bled when she'd shot him. He'd eaten food. He drew in breaths and exhaled them even now. She studied the way the pupils of his eyes flared as she stared at him and then contracted, making the green colors swirl.

"You are a man," she said. "A man." She repeated it several times because she needed to convince herself before he said anything to unravel the apparent thin grasp on reality that she had right then.

"Aye, a man, flesh and blood," he said back to her. He flexed his arm, the bandaged one, as if to prove he had blood in his body. The way he canted his head to one side just before he continued told Fee he was about to upend everything she believed. And then he did just that.

"A man now, but I have existed since Culloden, at Culloden, as a ghost."

Though the words should have unnerved her or frightened her—not the thought of a ghost but because she believed him—instead Fee felt a calmness fill her. She understood what was happening to her now. She released her hold on his hands and slid back against the wooden chair and nodded.

"A ghost," she said. "A ghost."

In that moment, she understood. She'd read about people who had died or were dying and the moments of clarity or vision they experienced. This was her moment of clarity, perhaps a chance to examine her conscience or review her life, before dying. Maybe she had fired the gun and had hit her target? Maybe she was dying or dead already? And like Dickens' *Christmas Carol*, he was the ghost sent to guide her through that?

Somehow, that made sense to her. Though in the movies and shows, the being looked like a ghost, this one retained his human appearance. Touching his hand for a second, she smiled. He also felt and looked alive.

"That explains a lot."

"It does?" he asked, frowning. He shook his head and shrugged and the movement drew her gaze down to his naked chest. He sat so close she could touch him if she wanted to.

"Your lack of knowledge about most things here. You cannot open a can or turn on the water." And his sudden appearance on the cliff. And his clothes. And his speech. And … and … and … She would have to suspend her every belief to accept this.

Or was he some kind of second chance for her? Sent to remind her of all she'd lost and would lose by ending her life? A way to cleanse her spirit before she passed? Whichever or whatever he was, Fee was aware of him in a way she'd not been aware of men since the accident. Not even Stephen affected her like this man did. Still …

"I must be having that moment," she said, watching his expression change from dark and serious to serious and confused. "That moment when your life flashes before you when you die. A moment to review your choices before you face …"

"The Almighty?" Fee swallowed deeply and nodded. "And ye think I am an examination of your conscience as ye die?"

"It's a better explanation than …"

"Better than what?"

"Well, better than I'm going stark raving mad and so is the stranger I've let in my house."

Silence swirled around them. Then, he leaned his head back and laughed loudly. God, but the sound of it sent chills through her. It was so natural and unforced. Not polite in the least, for he was laughing at her, but the way his body shook with it, well, it made her want to laugh, too.

Struan laughed until he thought his lungs would burst and as tears streamed down his face. He understood the lass was not trying to be funny or make light of her, their situation, but her dour expression as she spoke such an admission just made him laugh. He wiped the back of his hand across his face, coughed and then nodded.

"I ken that feeling, lass. I do." He pushed back on the wooden chair next to her and nodded. "When I awoke the morning after the battle and could see everything and everyone around me, but they couldna see or hear me, I thought I was mad, not dead."

Her lovely blue eyes startled then, meeting his gaze as he explained the lunacy of that day.

"I remember the sharpness of his blade as the sword hit my arm. I remember the blood, dear God, the blood. The field was soaked in it. Toward the end, 'twas hard to find a dry place to make a stand." Struan regretted the words as soon as he'd spoken them. The lass had a weakness about blood and here he was blathering on about it.

Looking away then, he continued to tell her of that day. How he'd trudged across that field yelling and waving with no effect. How he'd seen his friends and compatriots lying there, dead as he was but then not.

Then he made his admission, saying the words she needed to hear.

"Sometimes, I would be there. There on the moor, seeing and hearing things as clearly as I do now. I could see the others and, if I made myself concentrate, I could speak to them."

"Others?" she whispered, drawing his gaze back to her.

"I ken," he said, nodding at her discomfort. "I ken it sounds madder than my old Uncle Geordie, but I remember it all. There were seventy-nine of us left there on the moor after the battle cleared. Seventy-nine of us through all these years. And the worst of it all? I would speak and no' be heard. I would move but no' feel or be felt. No matter my actions, I was there and yet no'. I screamed once, trying to gain the attention of someone, anyone yet alive, but it did no' matter."

He dragged his hands through his unruly hair and rested against his palms. Nothing had mattered. Nothing they did in all the passing years changed or affected anything or anyone … but the young lass Soni.

Fiona's hand, warm and soft, on his arm surprised him then. With that small gesture, she reminded him of all he'd lost that day. And how much he missed this—the touch of another, the soft words of a woman, the concern of … He cleared his throat, trying to ease the tightness there.

"Mayhap we are indeed both mad?" he said softly. Even after he lowered his hands, hers remained there on his arm. Struan covered it with his and was somehow pleased when she did not pull away.

"Mad as old Uncle Geordie?"

"Och, aye. Him and his brother Dougal," he said. "They were born together and ended up the same way—daft in the head."

She smiled then. 'Twas the first he remembered seeing and it brightened her face so much it hurt him. No lass this lovely, this young, should be bereft of a smile or a laugh. He lifted his free hand and slowly reached out to touch her face. Struan moved slowly, waiting for a sign to stop, but none came.

With the edge of his finger, he touched her forehead and followed the curve of her cheek down to her chin. Her eyes drifted shut and he continued on. He did not trace the line of the scar, but instead, his finger glided around the edge of her face. Then, he touched the softness of her mouth, using the pad of his thumb, sliding it along the fullness of her bottom lip. That lip that drove him mad when it quivered or when she spoke.

"I am mad," he whispered as he leaned his head closer and touched his mouth to hers. She did not startle as he anticipated her to and so he rubbed his lips over hers. Good God, but they were as soft as he'd expected. He drew back and realized her eyes were no longer closed.

"What am I to do with you, Struan?" At that question, all sorts of things to do raced through his thoughts. And, to a one, they involved pleasures of the flesh—a thing also long denied him.

"What do ye wish to do, lass?" He'd uttered the words in a voice deepened with arousal. Her eyes flared then, not missing his meaning or his desire. "With me."

CHAPTER FIVE

Fee had never been an overly-intimate person. And maybe that was part of what drove Stephen away or, at least, made it easier for him to leave her. And yet, with little effort if any on his part, Struan Cameron made her blood boil. He did not hesitate as he touched her, even looking on her scars did not turn him away. His lips were warm and wonderful and she wanted more.

If they were both mad, she might be okay with it. If he was a ghost from a long-ago time and place, maybe it wasn't such a bad thing? Impossible and unbelievable, but not bad.

The danger was that, when this madness or reprieve from death ended, she would lose him as sure as she'd lost all the others. And she would face her end alone, once again. Whatever crazy desires surged through her ended at that realization and she straightened up away from him.

"I didna mean to overstep, lass." He smiled and she wanted to reach out and trace that mouth. He used the tip of his tongue then to lick his lower lip and it was mesmerizing to watch. "Ye looked like ye needed a kiss just then."

"I'm not sure what I need right now," she said, letting out a sigh. "I thought I knew. I thought I knew what I needed to do. But now? Not now." She shook her head and leaned back then, tugging her hand free and giving herself some space from this tempting man or ghost or whatever he was.

He watched her with an openness she could not decipher. He did not flinch at the coarse scars on her face as he touched them. There was no pity in his gaze. He did not rebuff her. Against her will and against all sense of self-protection, she wanted to know more about him. To understand why this was happening.

"And you? If you are a ghost, how did you come to be here and as you are?" She glanced down at that muscular chest briefly, too briefly if she had a choice, and then back up at his face. "Why are you here?"

"Soni sent me from the moor." He shook his head and spoke again. "Soni is a person with great powers. Somehow, she sent me back into my body and gave me two days to accomplish some task before …"

"Before?" She knew his answer as she asked the question.

"Before my soul can move on from this life, this time, this place."

"And you will be dead? *Dead* dead?"

"Ah, lass, ye have a way with words, ye do indeed. Aye, I will be truly dead."

He stood then and walked over to the door. With his height, it was easy for him to look out the window at the top of it. Though the night settled in early here in March, there was still enough light to see out. He turned the knob of the door and pulled it open, surprising her. "I will return."

"Where are you going?"

He blushed then. Somehow, it made him even more appealing and he looked younger, too. He stammered then and nodded toward the woods. She couldn't help but to smile then as she understood his situation.

"Let me show you," she said, standing and pointing down the hallway.

"Show me? Lass, truly I ken how to pish! Even if I havena needed to in almost three hundred years!"

His indignation was adorable. And somehow, it felt completely genuine to her. If he was or wasn't a ghost, it didn't matter really, for he believed it. If he was going to be here for only two days, what harm would there be in playing along with this? If she was in some state of limbo before dying, why not enjoy this time and discover the truth behind it?

"Of course, you do," she said, walking to the bathroom there. "But, you can see to it here and not worry about bears or other creatures that come out to hunt at night."

"Bears? Ye have bears here? There are no bears in Scotland," he said, walking close behind her. "I saw this room earlier. When you slept."

"Now that I know you don't know about modern plumbing and such, let me explain."

It took only a minute to explain the convenience of indoor plumbing before Fee left him alone. The toilet flushed several times and then a few more before Struan made his way back down to the kitchen and found her putting water on to boil for tea. He looked very happy with himself and he nodded to her.

"I like modern plumbing," he said. "Much more pleasant than the woods in the cold dark of night."

The absurdity of the whole situation—him, her, death, ghosts and peeing in a toilet—overwhelmed her then and she laughed.

And it surprised her for she'd not laughed in over three years. Not since all the joy had been ripped from her life in one moment of complete and utter destruction and anguish. The muscles of her face had forgotten how, but once she started, they learned again.

Tears flowed as she laughed and then she began coughing. He stood by, watching her closely but not interfering. When she finally could breathe again, Fee wiped her face with the back of her sleeve and realized she yet wore her coat.

And he wore only his pants.

"If you're going to be here for another day or two, you need some clothing. You can't run around like … this." And she could not continue to stare at this man's chest. The sight and his nearness of him prickled her senses. But it was more common courtesy that caused her to make her offer. "There's a storage chest in the bedroom upstairs. My father and my brother were … both big men. Something of theirs should fit you."

Her stomach clenched and Fee fought off the wave of grief. Strange how she felt more now than she had for months and months. Maybe the nearness of her own death was bringing it on? Well, she didn't like it at all. She'd escape it all soon enough. After her own personal *Twilight Zone* episode finished with Struan's departure, that was.

"Would they mind me borrowing their things, lass?" he asked.

She couldn't have answered if she'd wanted to. The words thickened in her throat and threatened to choke her.

So, Fee stood and walked on stiff legs to the stairs and climbed them, one at a time, struggling with each step. The sound of his breathing and the echoes of his paces told her that Struan followed closely. She reached the top and made her way to the last bedroom on the left. When she placed her hand on the light switch, she closed her eyes. The heat of him at her back pushed her on into the room of many memories.

"Here, take a look at these," she said, pointing to the large, cedar storage chest in the corner of the room. When she leaned down to open it, he eased around her and lifted the heavy lid without any apparent effort. "Any of those might work."

Fee stepped out of his way and let him search through the old work shirts and sweaters stored there. A mix of her father's and brother's clothes she'd moved into one place some time ago.

"And they wouldna mind me using their things?" The words were spoken so softly, she almost felt them ripple in the air rather than heard them.

"They're gone, Struan. All gone," she said, nodding to the photos displayed on the mantel there. "So, no, they would not mind."

Though he wanted to say or ask her something, he didn't. Instead he nodded and began checking the clothes. As he lifted different ones to size them up, she remembered a time she'd seen them worn. The blue flannel shirt her dad liked to wear while puttering around outside. A golf shirt he'd worn on his birthday. His robe, one that he'd had for years and one she'd wrapped around herself here when the grief was new and raw. She'd not washed it since and his smell wafted in the air when Struan shook it out.

"Ye are smiling." She glanced up to find him studying her. He folded the robe and placed it aside.

"My father wore that shirt when he was trying to fix a flat tire." She did smile then, remembering all the mishaps that prevented that bicycle tire from ever being repaired. He'd given up and just bought her a new bike instead.

"And this one?"

"Dad took my mom out in the canoe. Let's just say that didn't go well either."

He picked up one and then another, asking her each time to tell him about a moment, a memory, of her past. Of their past. When he reached the bottom of the trunk, he had a nice pile of possibles. Struan gathered them up and faced her.

"Will it bother ye if I wear these?" he asked, glancing at the shirts and sweaters and back at her.

Fee inhaled slowly, considering his question. "It will remind me of happier times, Struan. So, no, I won't mind if you do."

The sentiment was an honest one, for her heart did not hurt when she said the words. When he chose one and shook it out, she thought of another courtesy she could offer him.

"Have you ever taken a shower?"

CHAPTER SIX

A *rainforest showerhead*, the lass had called it.

He called it heaven on earth.

Though he'd been in the forest while rain poured down, never had it felt like this. Struan lifted his face once more to it and let the warm water cascade over his face and head and body. Whether the temperature of the water or the gentle way it sluiced over his skin, he knew not which was more pleasurable. He just enjoyed every single moment it did.

Washing in the cold streams or rivers had been his practice while in the army of the Bonnie Prince, just as every man did when he had the opportunity. He could not remember the last time he had a proper bath, or a warm one at that. Struan laughed then, realizing that much more time had passed than he'd given credit since he was last in the flesh in 1746.

Reaching out, Struan slid the knob as the lass had shown him and the water began to pelt down instead of the gentle fall before. He poured out a small amount of liquid soap and spread it over his hair and head. Bloody hell, it felt good to do this. And what a miracle this plumbing was! He'd thought that the toilet was one and then the lass had shown him this small enclosed bit of heaven. He would like to stay here forever.

Laughing, he finished washing and turned off the faucets and showerhead. He would have heard her sooner if he had not been so overwhelmed by the luxurious feel of the drying linens he used. Finally dressed in his trews and the borrowed sweater, he opened the door to the hallway and, at first, he heard nothing at all. The ticking of a clock. The call of a night bird outside. As he stepped into the hall, the soft sound happened.

Turning to and fro, he realized it came from one of the bedchambers there. He walked slowly, listening, hoping she'd stopped, until the next sob came from behind the door where he stood now. Such profound pain and loss in each cry. Struan ached for the deeply-held grief there within each sob and within this brave, sad lass. If he could only do something to ease her pain …

But he could.

Her loss was no different from his, not in its deepest measure. Time and place meant little to nothing. Whether lost in or to war or to other causes, the lives of our most precious ones cost her deeply, too. And just as he had for the other seventy-eight, his stories might help to ease her suffering. He could tell her the ones that would make her smile or, mayhap, laugh again. Struan eased the knob, opening the door slowly. As he expected, she held in her cries as he entered.

He said nothing at first and asked not permission for his approach. Walking to the bedside, he saw in the lowlight of some electrical candle that she lay in the center, curled up on her side, clutching something tightly to her chest.

The robe.

The one that made her eyes lose their brightness when she first saw it in the trunk. It must be dear to her to cause such pain and yet not be able to resist its call.

Without a word, he laid down next to her and slid his arm under her head and the other over her and the crumpled robe. She did not resist his movements, indeed, she allowed them and then leaned against him. His chest tightened as she continued to cry but over the next minutes, she stopped. A hiccup echoed through the air and he knew the worst was over. As he thought on which story to tell her, Soni's words came back to him.

Someone needs to hear yer stories now.

He'd changed his stories around when he told them on the moor, giving them much better endings than the real ones. Especially when he could tell that the others needed their spirits uplifted and a respite from their grief and hopelessness. Something told him now, though, that Fiona needed to hear his own story. One he'd not dared to speak in nigh on three hundred years.

"I left them in anger," he said, remembering the exact day his life had changed irreparably. "My clan rose for the rightful Stuart king, but not all were in favor of going off to fight for him or his son. My own father seemed to ken 'twas a bad idea and he forbade me to go." He let out a breath as the harsh words he'd spoken to his father echoed in his thoughts. "I had the arrogance of youth and inexperience and he was speaking words of wisdom, but I was too full of myself to take it in." For a moment, he thought she might have stroked his hand.

These memories were even more painful now that he was alive and made of flesh and blood, rather than the wisps of spirit and mist of these past centuries. Struan leaned his head down against the back of Fiona's, gaining comfort from her nearness.

"So, with others from my village, I left to follow

the Lochiel, my chieftain, and the prince. 'Twas not the glorious rising we all thought we'd see." He whispered now, unable to speak his fears aloud. "I saw so many die—of wounds and sepsis and hunger. I fought at Prestopans and Falkirk and I killed …"

He'd been a farmer, not a soldier or warrior, before the call went out from his chieftain. 'Twas war, the others had counselled him. 'Twas the way of things. But nothing had prepared him for the carnage he'd witnessed since he'd left his home. For losing so many kinsmen and friends.

"Word came after Falkirk of attacks more than four hundred farms and houses on Cameron lands and I got leave to travel home. 'Twas bad."

Whether the dread within him caused it or some other cause, Fiona tensed within his arms. Struan eased back a bit from her and loosened the hold he had on her. He wondered if he should skip further into his story when she spoke.

"Tell me, Struan. Tell me all of it." She turned in his arms a bit and pressed back against him.

"Troops under the orders of the Duke of Cumberland laid waste to my village and others along the loch. Houses, barns, farms, fields—all destroyed and burned to the ground." He swallowed then, against the pain that pierced him, heart and soul. "My father died trying to save my mother and my sisters from the flames."

The thought of those terrible deaths devastated him even now. How they died in terror. How they must have suffered. How they must have blamed him for not being there to help them.

"How many sisters did you have?"

"Three. I had three sisters."

He'd pushed these memories aside for centuries, not daring to dwell on the reasons behind his death. Or on his beloved sisters or parents. 'Twas too hard, really. Too hard to exist even in the mist of Drummossie when you thought too much about your life in flesh-and-blood. He told stories of many of his relatives, but none about those who were closest to him.

"My sister was named Sara," she whispered. "She was three years younger than me." He let out a breath at her admission, understanding what he must do then.

"Anna had ten years. Beatrice had twelve. And Cecelia had ten-and-four. When they died."

As he spoke their names aloud for the first time since their deaths, images of the three raced through his mind. The lasses racing along the edge of the loch, splashing and laughing as their mother called to them to have a care. The arguments that would flare among the three, all beautiful young women in the making. He'd forced those memories and so many more away, locked them deep inside himself and never allowed them to bother him. Not once since he'd died.

Well, not once since he made the decision to die.

The winds rose outside the cabin then, the first sign of an approaching storm, interrupting the silence that grew around them. Louder and louder, the winds increased and then, just as suddenly, the rains began, beating against the window next to the bed. It happened quickly, just as it did in Scotland—very little, if any, warning and it was on top of you.

They lay there together, with the storm raging around them outside and a similar one swirling inside him. To tell the rest, to honestly tell the rest, he would reveal his own greatest sin. Though Fee thought him to be a moment to examine her conscience, Struan considered that it was possible she was his.

And, perchance, this was the reason he was here, now, with Fiona—a woman who was about to commit the same grievous sin that he had? For he had not returned to the field to kill the men who served those responsible for his family's destruction. Nay, he had returned to die. To let them kill him and put an end to his misery and shame.

Well, if this was the purpose of Soni's magic, to give him this chance at absolution before facing the Almighty, he'd not waste it. The room was chilly now, so he eased away from her to grab the blanket that lay folded at the bottom of the bed. Tossing it over both of them, he smiled as she lifted her head and let him draw in close. He liked the feel of her in his arms. He enjoyed her softness and curves against him.

In all the years existing as ghost, he'd not once lamented over the loss of pleasures of the fleshly kind. Strange that, since most of those who'd risen that day and those who yet waited on the moor were in their prime. Young men all, but for the one called Eight, who was younger than any of them and truly, just a lad.

Now, though, laying in her bed, his limbs and body wrapped around her, Struan remembered the joys that could be had by a man and a woman. Trying to fight the attraction of her and the distraction that would draw him from what he believed was his challenge, Struan cleared his throat and told her the rest.

He told her the worst.

His grave sin that was an affront to God and to good people. The same one that she had attempted on the cliff.

"I only returned to Lochiel's men because I lacked the courage to do what you've been planning to do, Fiona," he whispered then. "I wanted to die but could not take my own life. So, I went into battle with no intention of surviving it."

He heard and felt the quick inhalation of surprise in her. Struan thought she might speak but she did not. And he could not tell if she had simply been surprised by his words or disgusted by his lack of bravery.

"By some mistake, the Lochiel's men on the right

flank charged before the left one did and it took us directly to Barrel's and Munro's regiments and the thick of the fighting. I thought it would be easy to die that day. But, something in me would not give up. I fought until I saw Lochiel taken down by grape shot. If my chieftain was down, I thought 'twas time."

He explained it all even as the sights and sounds swirled in his thoughts—he could hear the roar of the Highlanders' charge and smell the powder of the guns and the cannon around him then. The charge turned into screams and wailing as more and more of them were cut down there on the moor. When one soldier ran at him, brandishing his sword, Struan dropped his arms to his side and paused for one brief moment.

The slice that took his arm off at the shoulder, the injury that would take his life, was quick and less painful than he thought it would be. It took less time and less effort than he expected to die.

"And that is how I died—of my own free will. Because I could not stand the thought of living without them. Because I chose to die that day."

The only thing he could hear when he finished his admission, his confession, was their breathing, his still racing and hers slow and calm. She lifted his hand and entwined their fingers together before pressing it to her cheek … her tear-dampened cheek.

They lay there with no words to say as the storm outside blew hard against the cottage and the trees.

The sound of that chaos somehow calmed the one within him and soon Struan found himself being lulled into sleep.

CHAPTER SEVEN

The soundness and depth of her sleep surprised her. Fee opened her eyes to find daylight streaming into the small window that faced the east. And she found herself alone in that bed. She'd never even felt his departure. That was not normal.

Fee would admit that she hadn't shared a bed with anyone in a long time and the last time she slept with a man, well, that was long ago, too. Yet, for a while in the middle of the night, he'd been wrapped around her so tightly and she savored that closeness. When she'd awakened in the dark, she could not feel a place where a skosh of space separated his body from hers. The truly strange thing was that she'd not slept soundly in years and yet she'd slept through his leaving the bed and the room.

Rolling onto her back, Fee began the stretching exercises that started every day of her life before she would even think about getting up. This morning, they seemed easier and her body was still warm, not cold or shivering as she usually woke.

From having his body wrapped around her through the night.

There had been a moment when he'd embraced her and all of his strength and heat poured into her and, for that moment, she'd not felt as alone and separate as she had for years. As she climbed from the bed, she realized she'd slept in her clothes. But the sight of her father's robe, there on the bed even now, had torn her heart in pieces in an unexpected way. Oh, showing Struan his sweaters and shirts twisted her gut but that robe was a killer for her.

In only a few minutes, she washed and changed and went downstairs to find Struan. The house's silence told her he was not there. Had he gone? Had telling his story to her finished whatever he must do to leave? She quickened her steps through the living room and kitchen and spoke his name.

No one answered.

Well, she was back on her own and now must either move forward with her plan or accept that she'd failed. Lost in her thoughts, she moved around the kitchen and she only noticed that she was making tea when the electric kettle boiled. A habit of long standing that. Her parents and sister preferred coffee while she and Ian were tea drinkers. But their practice was first-up, make-the-coffee-tea.

Oh, dear God, how she wanted to make coffee for them again!

If only she hadn't called the family meeting at the office to discuss a new venture. If only it hadn't been THAT day. If only they'd heard the whistling of the gas building beneath their feet. If only … If only.

Pain unlike anything she'd felt in months pierced her heart, forcing her to grab hold of the counter to stay on her feet. The guilt. The knowing that her actions had resulted in her family's death. Everyone tried to convince her otherwise, telling her that there were thousands or millions of variables that all came together in that place, in that moment, on that day. Those variables caused their deaths, they said. Not her. But Fee knew the truth—she'd failed to have the furnace serviced a month before when the leak would have been discovered and corrected.

The officials said it was an accident. The inspectors said it could have happened at any moment. But they didn't know. They didn't know how she'd failed. She stood there, mired in the misery that had controlled her since that day, barely able to breathe around the pain.

Tires crunching on the dirt of the road outside her

cabin pulled her from the grasp of reliving the past. A car or truck pulled up and stopped in front of her door. Walking to the front door, she heard Struan's voice calling out.

"Good day to ye, Matt! And my thanks for bringing me back!"

As she opened the door, Struan slammed the truck's door and tapped on the roof. Matt, who owned the general store a few miles down the road, nodded and waved at both of them and drove off. Struan stood there with a bag in each hand, smiling and nodding himself.

"You went shopping?" Her own stomach grumbled then, surprising her since she was rarely hungry.

"Aye. Well, nay. I went off to walk by the sea, got turned around on the path and ended up south of here," he said as he passed her. Carrying the bags into the kitchen, he began emptying the contents on the counter. "I'd walked a few miles when I came to the main road and saw Matt's market store."

A dozen eggs. A pound of bacon. A small bottle of cream. An unsliced loaf of bread, probably Janet's, probably made this morning. Smaller packages of sliced deli meats, from the look of them. The essentials. The last thing he took out was a bottle of wine.

"Matt was surprised that you were here, but I

explained it was an unplanned visit and only for another day and that your cupboard was bare. He said he'd put this on yer bill."

She smiled at his words. "The wine?"

"Och, aye," Struan said, holding out the bottle to her. "Matt said it's a new vineyard from over on Serenity Harbor and he wanted ye to give it a try."

"You seem to have found your way around here," she said, smiling at his expression.

"Ye were sleeping so soundly, I didna wish to wake ye," he said. "I needed to get some air, so I began walking. Ye ken the rest." He glanced out the window that overlooked the back porch, looking for … something. "I can cook if ye wish to break our fast."

"You cook?" she asked. He arched a brow at her and she suspected he did indeed know how to cook. If his story was true, he needed to be self-sufficient during the time he was on the road with the Bonnie Prince's army. They did not have the modern warfare or army practices to rely on and so he knew how to cook. Probably whatever food he found or killed or could buy.

"If ye have a girdle pan, I can make a fire outside," he suggested. "Or if ye show me how this cooking … *stove* works, I am certain I can figure it out."

He stepped out of her way as she opened one of the closets beneath the cooktop and pulled out a *griddle* pan. Placing it over the grill top section of the stove, she turned on the flames under it and motioned him closer.

"This is on low heat now. Turn this," she pointed at the correct knob, "to turn the heat up."

Fee moved to the counter where the kettle waited and made two of the largest mugs of tea she could. With sugar and a dollop of the cream he'd brought back, Fee was content that it was also the perfect cup of tea. She placed his next to the stove where he could reach it. Before he did anything else, he got a chair from the table, placed it there and nodded. "Sit."

So, she did. Fee found herself both entertained and amazed by his efficient and proficient cooking skills. And she found herself studying this stranger who'd walked, ran, into her life and now was making breakfast for her. More than that, he made it all feel so … *normal.* Like finding a tall, handsome, sexy Highlander ghost now flesh-and-blood in her kitchen happened every day.

He'd pulled his shoulder-length hair back into a ponytail, tied and held out of his face. He must have washed it last night during his shower and slept with it wet, for she could see his reddish-brown curls struggled to be free of the control of the ponytail. He wore the same sweater now, over his own pants, and he slid the sleeves up on his forearms to keep them out of his way. Fee had not really taken notice of a man's forearm before, but the sprinkling of dark auburn hair appealed to her.

As usual, he began to tell her stories—stories about cooking mishaps in his family and along the path to Culloden and she stopped fighting her amusement and laughed along with him. Soon, the kitchen filled with the delicious aroma of bacon frying and the appealing sound of his Scottish-accented voice. He had a methodical approach to making the meal—first the bacon fried, then he dipped thick slices of Janet's fresh bread into the grease and let them grill. So much for heart-healthy cooking! When the bread was fried and crispy, he moved it aside and broke a series of eggs onto the griddle. Rather than scrambling them in a separate bowl, he used a fork and the spatula to mix them as they cooked. Again, efficient.

And her mouth watered waiting for him to finish.

Getting plates from the cabinet, she held them out to him and he divided the food between them. Struan took the plates to the table and waited for her to join him there. Fee almost moaned at the taste of the bread when she bit into it. From Struan's laugh, Fee understood that she'd made the sound loud enough for him to hear.

"I am pleased that ye like the food," he said, between bites of egg and bacon and fried bread.

"It's all wonderful."

"'It'll do to fill yer belly', my mam would say." He

scooped up the last of the eggs on his plate and held them up. "Aye, they'll do."

Once the dishes were cleaned and put away, he reached out for her hand. Fee hesitated but he simply held his out there, waiting for her to relent. And she did.

"Come outside, lass. 'Tis the most beautiful day after a storm I've seen in a long time."

Whether it was that enticing accent or voice, or the man himself or the invitation, she could not tell which of the temptations made her succumb. He led her to the kitchen door and opened it. He was right—a gentle breeze of cool, fresh air rushed inside, filling the room with the clean scent of the ocean after a storm. Grabbing a jacket from the peg there, she walked with him outside. They reached the edge of the property, he stopped.

"I thought it would never stop last night. The rain pounding on the house and the windows. The winds, by God, the winds were so high!" He smiled at her. "I was tempted to walk out in it. To feel it on my skin once more."

"How did you live that way without going mad?"

He startled at her question then, searching her face and meeting her gaze. "That almost sounded as though ye believe me."

She turned to face him and lifted her hand free. "I think I do." Fee glanced at her hand before dropping it to her side. "I do." She swallowed and nodded at the small patio nearby. "You told me a bit about how it felt. What the others were like."

"I will tell ye only if ye tell me yer story, Fiona Masters."

Her lovely eyes emptied for a scant moment and then fear crept in, darkening them. He believed she would refuse. She'd said almost nothing about what had brought her to the cliffside and, other than what he'd observed himself, he still had little idea of her motives for ending her life.

Loss? Oh, clearly she had lost those she loved the most. But many people did without wanting to end their lives. Was it for her as it had been for him—had she played some part in their deaths and the guilt of it drove her to the cliff with a gun in her hand? Nay, that could not be.

Did she think to go through with it after Soni came and fetched him? Did she mayhap need a moment to unburden her conscience? Had there been no priest for her? They'd had priests on the battlefield, to bless those fighting and to hear confessions, but Struan had not dared to speak to a priest about his decision.

"Fine." The whispered word floated on the breeze between them.

He nodded and stood. "I'll bring ye some tea."

He did not wish to delay, but he wanted to see to her comfort as she did speak. 'Twas clear to him that she had no one to see to her and that she suffered much from whatever had injured her. So, he watched through the kitchen window as she settled in one of the chairs there on the *patio* as she called it. He freshened their cups and carried them out. After handing her one, he sat gently into another chair, hoping it would hold him up. It was not wood nor any metal he'd seen before and he held little confidence in its light frame to remain upright. Then, he waited for her to speak, knowing he could not force the words from her. When she did, he nearly fell over, chair and all.

"I killed my whole family."

Chapter Eight

"Ye killed yer family?" He shook his head and righted himself and the flimsy chair under him. "I canna believe that, lass."

She said nothing else for a long time and they sat quietly with only the sounds of the winds rustling through the trees and a few sea birds screeching out in the distance.

"If ye are not ready, should I tell ye more about being a ghost?" He thought that if he began first, it might ease her way. When she replied neither aye nor nay, he went on. "I told ye about rising the next morn with the others and how we could not seem to make ourselves known to those on the battlefield." He watched her closely for any reaction. At her slight nod, he went on. "I do not remember much about the passage of time, just that it did. Sometimes, we would gather together—"

"And you would tell your stories?"

"Aye. Sometimes, aye. Other times, we were simply there. We would trail after visitors to the fields, once that became something that people did. The first two centuries, we had it mostly to ourselves once the English and their supporters cleaned the field." He shivered then, at memories of watching the Butcher's soldiers move in waves across the battlefield. "They used their bayonets or swords on any fallen man or boy that might not be dead yet. He earned his name beginning that day, I will tell ye. 'The Butcher.' Duke of Cumberland, the king's son." He paused and spit on the ground as the name passed his lips.

"You? Did they do that to you?" she asked.

"Nay, lass. I was clearly dead to anyone looking. But it wouldna mattered for I could not survive my injury." He couldn't help but reach up and rub his shoulder and arm, one he was still not accustomed to having back.

"And you never knew why you'd been left there as spirits?"

"Nay." He drank down the rest of his tea and shook his head. They'd talked about it over the years and none could think of any reason they had been left behind when others moved on.

"We had nothing in common other than we fought for the line of James, the rightful king of Scotland. We came from different clans, different septs, and different places." He met her gaze across the distance and he knew the question she most wanted to ask. Fiona put her cup down on the table there.

"How does it feel to die, Struan? That is what I want to know."

"Nay, lass. Ye want to ken what happens after the dying."

"And that, too."

"I only can tell ye about dying, Fiona. And only my story, for that is one thing that we never talked about on the moor."

"Did it hurt?" she asked. "Not the injury, of course. But the dying?"

"Only my arm hurt. Only my arm." He shook his head as he rubbed the length of it again. "I saw his approach and his weapon held high. He was no taller than me and not much older but he put his weight behind the stroke and it took only the one blow to take my arm."

She shivered now and he was tempted to stop. But, if he was to hear her words, she must hear his.

"I fell to the ground and I could feel the cold begin to move up from my feet as my blood poured out. The icy chill numbed me until it reached my heart. The last beat was no different from the other thousands I'd felt before. Then, nothing. I dinna remember closing my eyes and yet, darkness covered me. The screams and the calls dissipated until there was only silence."

"You felt nothing else?"

"Nay. Then, the next thing I remember was being aware of the moor again. I opened my eyes and stood, except that my body remained there on the ground."

"Did you try to leave the moor?"

Struan stood then and walked to the edge of the paved floor beneath his feet. Staring off into the forest, he shrugged and answered.

"We did try. No one could. If we tried, we simply faded away as we did when we did not try to stay."

"So, you spent your time telling your stories to entertain them?"

"Not at first, nay. We watched as the land and the people changed. It took months for the battleground to be cleared and for all the bodies to be buried. It hurt to watch then—emotions seemed stronger and rose easier then. Over time, feelings faded and it took too much effort to raise them. Except the darker emotions. Fear, anger, desolation, despair, sadness—they came quickly and easily and remained far too long as our companions."

"Oh Struan," she said. Her sorrow for him touched him more than anything had in his life. "To remain like that … it must have been terrible. No wonder you told your stories."

"I canna even remember when I told my first story.

Or even which one it was. But one and then another would ask me to, and I would. Sometimes I made them laugh. Other times, I just tried to ease their suffering and make them … less anxious."

"Did you tell stories over and over? I guess there were favorites that they liked to hear?"

"I might have taken some liberties with the one about the battle itself." He laughed then and met her gaze. "I changed the outcome to one we all wanted. In various ways, with different charges and ploys, but always we were victorious."

"Did it help?" She sat up now on the edge of her chair, interested more than he'd witnessed in the last day of their conversations and encounters.

"Aye," he said. "I think it did. More so at different times." Struan walked to her now and held out his hand once more. "Come, would ye like to walk a bit and tell me what ye ken ye wish to say?"

Fiona looked as though she would refuse, for her chin took on a stubborn tilt and she straightened her shoulders back. Then, she pushed herself up to her feet and nodded.

"I would like to take a walk. The day can turn cold and rainy so quickly in the autumn here, so it's a shame if we don't take advantage of it."

"'Tis much like that in the Highlands. The spring and autumn are the most unpredictable."

He noticed that, though she'd spoken on the safe

topic of the weather, she'd still said nothing about talking to him and telling her story, but Struan decided not to pressure her. From all she'd said and from what Matt had told him, she did not need pressure. As she stood, he followed her to the path that led to the ocean.

So, someone had sent her a kindred spirit rather than a cantankerous or argumentative one. The more he spoke of his life and his death and his stories, Fee understood that their lives and losses had led them to a similar ending. Or, in her case, an attempted one. In her opinion, he was the perfect person to whom to tell the truth, the whole truth.

If this was her moment of clarity, then, so be it.

They'd walked just a short distance on the path when he held out his arm. She took hold as they moved along, heading toward the ocean. This path was a different one and it would take them downhill to a small clearing that was closer to the beach. And even if it was a smoother, easier surface and not as hard for her to keep her balance, Fee held onto his strong arm anyway.

It didn't take them long to reach the clearing, not with his support. She'd noticed that he'd shortened his stride to match hers and let her set their pace. Long legs like his would cover the distance much faster than hers. She remembered staring at his legs in those tight pants and could feel a blush creep up on her cheeks. If he noticed that, he said nothing of it.

The clearing was just that, a small, almost-circular area without trees which sat overlooking the beach below. The scene of many private and romantic moments in her family happened in this place. Arguments, too. This was where Steve proposed to her that summer before everything in her life changed irreparably.

"Here, sit," Struan said, easing her over to one of the huge boulders that lay strewn around the edge. "Ye did well, lass." Somehow, the way he called her 'lass' warmed her heart. That accent and voice didn't hurt either.

"Thank you for your help. I can't remember making it this far so smoothly in a long time."

She released his arm and he moved away. He crossed his arms over his chest and nodded in reply to her thanks.

"Not since the accident then?"

Fee let out a sigh. Either it was a good guess or Matt, the local gossip, had told him what had happened. "Matt?" she guessed.

"Aye. Matt. Though he did not say much. He seemed to guard yer privacy as if ye paid him to do so."

"Yet he brought you back to the cabin and put groceries on my bill." Matt and Janet were so soft-hearted, she didn't doubt that they would have done that for him even if he'd not used her name. "What did you tell them?"

"Me? I said only that I was staying with ye on this unexpected trip and that ye needed some supplies."

Oh gosh, they must have thought Struan was a new boyfriend she'd brought from the city. "What did they say to that?" She smiled then, imagining how they must have almost salivated over this juicy tidbit of gossip they could share with the other residents.

"Well, Matt said 'twas about time and that I should enjoy the weekend." He paused and looked over at her with a very uncomfortable expression on his face. "Janet, well, Janet got a bit teary and told me that we should just be happy."

Fee's eyes teared then and her throat grew tight. "They're good people."

"They care about ye, lass." He sat next to her then and she eased over on the rock so he could fit there. "So, tell me about the accident."

"I'm sure they told you the details."

"Nay. They said nothing of it. Just referred to it—'since the accident,' and so on." He settled next to her, his warmth already seeping into her body where they touched. "When did it happen?"

"Three years, two months, one week and … four days ago."

He made a sound then, kind of a soft exhalation out

of his nose, that seemed to say he was surprised by her precise measure of time passed and yet not. He nudged her lightly. "Go on then."

The words poured out faster than she'd expected. Something in the way he held in any comments and questions and only seemed to wait on her made it easier to tell the horrible story.

"Do you know anything about me? My family?" she asked. She'd not thought about that until just now.

"Nay, lass. Only what ye have shared with me. Yer name, yer sister's name."

"My family owns several businesses. Owned." She owned them all now. "I ran one of them out of a condo that serves as our headquarters in Boston." She waited for his reaction to that but he didn't move or speak. "I'd called them all to a meeting about some plans I'd been making. Expansion. Development. Changes. And I wanted their approval even if I didn't need their permission."

"Ye could do such things on yer own then?" he asked.

"Yes. I could."

"Good for ye, lass." She felt the approval in those small words all the way into her soul. It didn't make sense that this stranger's words meant so much, but they did.

"No one knew that gas was leaking from the heater

below us. No one heard or smelled anything until it exploded."

"Good God Almighty!" he whispered as he wrapped his arm around her shoulders and held her. "It must have been terrible."

Coming from a man who'd faced the cannons of war on battlefields, it made her realize the true situation. She'd lived through it, but remembered almost nothing of the moments after the horrendous sound and the blast of heat and light engulfed them all.

"I have no memory of the days and weeks after the blast. Most of the surgeries needed to save my life or piece me back together were done in those empty days. They told me that everyone but my sister and me died instantly. She didn't make it past the first day."

"So, 'twas yer parents, yer sister and brother and ye?"

"And two of our staff secretaries and a custodian who was cleaning upstairs."

He reached out and wiped across her cheek with a gentle motion. Tears. He was wiping her tears.

"So ye had no one to help ye? No one to have a care for ye?" She choked at his words then and on the tears, on the memories, and the loss.

"My fiancé helped. At first."

Struan released her and turned to face her. "Ye are betrothed? Then where is the bastard now if not at yer side in a time of such dire need?"

CHAPTER NINE

She wanted to kiss this man. She wanted to throw her arms around him and hug him so hard for his disgruntled anger at a man he did not know. Angry on her behalf. No one had ever expressed anything but understanding for Steve and the broken engagement just two months after her release from the hospital for the final time.

No one had understood her needs. He'd boasted about an offer of a better job in New York City and how she needed to focus on her recovery. It had sounded caring and concerned but the man did not care for anyone but himself. He did not want to have to wait around and he did not want to wait on her. Her physical therapy and emotional support would be too hard for him.

Fee had been too weak and torn apart and devastated to realize it at the time. But, that revelation was one of few good ones she'd had in all the counseling that followed.

Struan stood then and took a few steps away before looking at her.

"He is no man if he would desert ye at a time like this," he said, anger infusing every word. Then, he spit on the ground at his feet and shook his head. "No man at all."

Once more she was struck with the urge to run to him and hug him. Instead, the untimely need that bubbled up from deep within her could not be controlled. She laughed then, a loud, inappropriate laugh that had the man staring at her across the clearing.

"I am sorry, Struan. I didn't mean to laugh. It's just that no one in all this time has ever taken my side. No one thought him the bad guy in our situation. I had myself convinced that I did not deserve him."

"Aye, lass. Ye have the right of it—ye did not deserve such a lack-witted, milk-sop, self-centered cur as that. Thank the Almighty ye are not saddled with him in matrimony." He stopped then and his expression went blank. "Oh, Holy Mother of Christ, tell me ye didna marry the bastard!"

Fee did it again. She laughed until all the muscles in her face and stomach hurt. When he approached her, still staring quite seriously at her and waiting for an answer, she held up her hand and shook her head.

"No! I am not married to him."

"Weel, thank the Almighty," he said as he sat down at her side. "That would have been a mistake not easily undone." He lifted her hand in his and stroked it with his thumb, his motions gentle and soothing. "I beg yer pardon for losing my temper, lass." He leaned in closer and spoke in a softer tone. "Why is he not here by yer side, easing yer burdens and helping ye during yer troubles?"

She stared at the movements of his thumb on her scars there and knew the truth—this man would have died with his family if he'd been there. He would have fought to his death to protect them. Loyalty shone in his gaze and Fee understood right then and there, that her story would have had a different ending if she'd met a man like him instead of Stephen Richards.

"He chose himself over me. Simple as that," she admitted. "When I survived but was injured and not perfect according to his standards, he found excuses not to stay." She let out a sigh then and shrugged. "I thought if one more surgery could repair the damage, if one more treatment or therapy could restore me, he would stay and love me."

"Bastard." He whispered the word under his

breath, but she heard it and it made her smile again. "Ye lived through hell, lost everyone and he left ye. My mam would say 'better to leave the rubbish behind than to carry it in yer pocket.'"

"I think I would have liked your mother."

Struan smiled back and nodded. "Aye."

They sat silently for a few minutes, with only the sound of the relentless crashing of the waves on the rocks and beach around them. The lochs where he'd lived could get quite wild and rough but never like the ocean did. He'd visited his uncle who lived out on one of the islands and found himself completely under the spell of the motion of the waves.

"Ye have not spoken of why ye are responsible for their deaths."

Her body reacted, he could feel the way she began to pull away from him then, but he refused to allow it. He held her hand firmly until she gave up trying. His thumb traced the web of scars then. He'd noticed the motion seemed to ease her in some way.

"I called them there that day."

"This explosion? It could have happened at any time?"

"Yes, but I brought them there when we could have spoken at home. And …"

Struan comprehended that her next words were the heart of the matter. He'd never truly confessed his own guilt in his family's death to her but she was about to reveal hers to him.

"I was in charge of overseeing the maintenance of the heater. I'd ignored the reminders from the service company. They'd warned me that cleaning and … upkeep was long overdue." She met his gaze then and he read the guilt there. "If I had done my job, they'd still be alive today."

"Fiona—"

"It's true, Struan. Instead, I'm the one who caused it and yet I'm the only one alive."

He'd thought on this very matter a lot over the passing years and centuries. If he'd been home, he could have saved his parents. He could have saved the wee ones. The only thing that consoled him at first was the fact that he was dead. He had died to pay for his sins, even if he'd accomplished it by his own actions. He'd not been alive and breathing while his kin moldered in their graves.

But Fiona Masters lived with her grief and guilt and it would kill her, even if she did not take her own life with her own hands. For she suffered from the same delusion he had—that he could have stopped the fate of his loved ones.

The same belief that filled survivors long after the devastation or loss they'd experienced. He'd heard the cries and prayers of those who'd survived the battle and made their way back to the battlefield when it was safe to do so in the years after the battle and the

Hanoverian's vengeance on the Highlands and Highlanders for supporting the Pretender's claim to the throne.

Sometimes they came alone, furtively like thieves in the dark of night. They would walk the field like the ghosts did. Always back to a place they remembered—where they'd lost kith or kin in the terrible throes of fighting. Sometimes they brought someone with them. But always, always, they confessed their guilt that they should have died that day on the moor.

Much later, the descendants of the clans that stood for the Bonnie Prince would visit and even erect monuments and cairns of remembrance to those who died. That too struck Struan as a sense of guilt. When visitors and tourists arrived, he would hear them discussing other possible outcomes. If only this happened or if that clan or another rose in support or if the French did this or that. Centuries of guilt over actions or inaction.

And though he'd felt the same way about his family's destruction, the other ghosts did not. Instead they carried other regrets about what they would miss … or rather who they missed.

Now, recognizing the same guilt in the eyes of this lovely, brave lass, he could offer her counsel much as he had to the other ghosts through his stories. But not with a story … just the truth.

"And, if ye had died there that day, would it bring yer loved ones back?" The words pierced him as he spoke them for they were him as well. "Would yer family had wanted ye to die with them that day?"

She jerked as if he'd slapped her. Blinking several times against the tears he saw gathering there, she began to answer him several times and was unable to speak the word.

"Nay, lass. They wouldna. Ye ken it as I ken that my family would not have wanted me to die with them. They loved ye. They love ye even now."

"But I ..." She stopped and wiped at her eyes with her sleeve. "If I ..."

"If ye had done whatever, would it have mattered? Did ye choose the day of their deaths? Only the Almighty can do that. And clearly, ye were not meant to die that day."

"But why? Why am I still here when they are all dead?"

Something within him let go then. The guilt he'd been carrying for centuries released its hold on his heart and soul as he spoke the words he finally accepted and that she must hear.

"Because ye were not meant to die that day, Fiona. There is still some task undone that ye must see to before 'tis yer time."

"It's too painful to live without them, Struan. You know that." Her blue eyes searched his face. "And what purpose can there be for a nearly-crippled, scarred woman who cannot even aim the gun she meant to use to kill herself?"

"The scars are marks of yer battle, yer successful battle, against death. Do not worry over them, lass. They proclaim yer victory. Yer power."

She startled then as he lifted their joined hands up and kissed hers. He released it and turned it to place his lips on the worst one and kissed it. She would have spoken then, but he placed his finger on her mouth to stop her. He was not done.

"And I suspect that, even if ye didna die three years, two months, one week and four days ago, ye did stop living. Once ye forgive yerself, ye will find a purpose to make ye want to live."

"What about you, Struan? If you survived the attack that killed your family, what was your purpose?"

He stood then and tugged her to her feet. Pulling her close, he wrapped his arms around her. He felt her hands move around him and grab hold of the sweater he wore. It felt right, holding her like this.

"Mayhap this was my purpose? I did not die with my family so that I could die on Drummossie Moor that day and be caught up in this bigger plan? So, after a time in purgatory itself, I could be sent here to make ye see that ye do not have to make the mistake I did?"

When she lifted her face to his and met his gaze,

Struan did what he'd wanted to do since the first moment. He leaned down until he could feel her breath against his lips and kissed her. This remarkable, beautiful, strong, brave woman who thought herself not worthy to live. He kissed her deeply, truly and with a new passion he had not felt before.

"I pray ye not to make the same mistake I did, Fiona Masters."

Struan kissed her with all the hope he'd had before taking the first step that set his course. He kissed her as a man does a woman he wants. He kissed her because not kissing her was not possible. When he finally lifted his mouth from hers, they were both breathless. She reached up and touched his face then, sliding her hand along his brow and cheek and jaw as if to memorize the shape of it.

"Come. Let's go back inside," he whispered. "The winds have turned and a storm is building again."

He released her and took her hand in his, placing hers across his body on his right arm and encircling her with his left arm. In this moment, he did not want to lose the feel of her against him. They walked out of the clearing and toward the cabin slowly, never letting go of the other. When the cabin came into view, Struan stopped there and took a breath.

"To understand, I must confess that I didna tell ye the whole truth, Fiona." She tensed in his arms, trying to ready herself for another blow.

"In those last moments on the battlefield, when my lifeblood drained away, I kenned I'd made a terrible mistake. I kenned that I'd been a coward choosing an easy death over a hard life. My last thought was that I wanted to live."

"You did?"

"Aye. In that moment, I prayed for forgiveness. I prayed for my family. I prayed for life." He shrugged then. "'Twas too late for me, but 'tis not too late for ye."

Struan turned back toward the cabin and only then noticed that they were being watched.

"Who are you?" Fiona asked of the young woman who stood there in the shadows of the trees watching them.

"Hello, Soni," he said. "'Tis over then?"

CHAPTER TEN

A woman wearing a long black coat stood there staring at them. Had she been following them? Had she witnessed that kiss? As the woman approached them now, Fee saw that she was only a teenager. And it was not a coat she wore as much as a cloak that almost touched the ground as she walked.

"Storyteller?" the girl said to Struan. "Was I right?"

For some reason, the girl seemed to glow. A faint green glimmer seemed to ebb and flow around her. Fee rubbed her eyes to try to clear them. The glow remained, and actually it grew stronger with each step closer.

"Aye, Soni," he said. He glanced over at Fee and

nodded. "I think my stories gave her ease from her pain."

"Not yer stories, Struan," Soni said.

"My story." Struan seemed shaken by that admission as much as he had by the confession of his change of heart.

"Wait, she told you that when?" Fee looked from one to the other and realized who this girl must be. "This is the powerful person you said sent you here?"

"Aye, Fiona. I sent him to ye, lass." This girl spoke with the same burr in her voice as Struan.

"Soni is a Muir witch."

Fee wanted to scoff but how could she with all she'd seen and heard so far?

"And now what?" she asked. "You take him back? Make him a ghost again?" Something she'd not felt in a long time rose within her, making her voice a bit sharp.

Anger.

"You sent him here to save me and now you will make him die?" This was her worst nightmare all over again. Another person would die because of her. "You taunted him with this short time as a man again and will tear it all away from him. Because of me?"

"Fiona," he said as he took a step to her side. "I already died, lass. This just ends it all."

"Say yer farewells, Storyteller," Soni said softly, never answering Fee's questions. "'Tis time to go."

Fee went into his embrace without a second thought. And the kiss, well, she didn't think about that either. He wrapped her in his arms and she felt his warmth and strength surround her. She could stay here forever … Too soon the kiss and the embrace were done and he let her go.

"Remember, ye are worth living, Fiona Masters. Do not make the mistake I did and realize it too late," he whispered.

"Struan, I …" She could not say anything to him, but … "Thank you."

"Yer welcome, lass." He leaned in for one more too-quick, too-quickly-done kiss and stepped away from her.

Her personal Christmas Carol experience was over and the ghost sent to give her time to examine her conscience and her path was leaving. He'd taken a few paces toward the girl when she called out to him.

"Struan, you never told me what number you were." It was a small thing but she knew it would bother her later when she remembered these last twenty hours and thirty minutes with him. "What number are you?"

"Seven, lass. I was the seventh to rise from the moor the day after the battle."

The green glow brightened with every step he took toward the girl. As Fee watched, Soni reached out to Struan.

"No." Fee shook her head and took one step and then another. "No!" she called out just before Soni touched him. The girl looked at her.

"It is not fair, Soni. He has seen to all the others for two hundred and fifty …"

"Two hundred sixty-nine years, six months and twenty-three days," Struan said. Fee could not help but smile at the way he imitated her counting of the days since her accident.

"He has helped them, telling stories, ignoring his own pain, to see to theirs," she said. "Shouldn't someone take care of him for a change?"

"And ye? Ye are offering to have a care for him when ye canna even see to yer own needs?" Soni asked. "I dinna think ye can, Fiona Masters."

The girl was right. She could barely live on her own. She could not drive herself and had not worked in more than three years. She had no right to interfere with whatever was happening here.

Then, she met his eyes and saw there a glimmer of something that looked like hope and she knew the path she must take.

"I will try." She stood up to her full height and nodded. "I will try."

"What say ye, Struan Cameron? Do ye wish to stay here or do ye wish to seek the revenge ye were promised?" Soni asked.

"'Twould seem the lass wants me to stay, Soni. Ye

sent me here to stop her from ending her life and I did that." Struan's gaze did not waver or break from hers then. He nodded. "I would stay, if 'twas possible. Aye, I would."

Just when Fee thought it might work out as she wanted, Soni shook her head.

"What about making the one responsible for all the losses ye and the others suffered pay the cost of his ambitions?"

"I chose to leave my family and follow the prince, Soni. I chose to fight for him. We are each responsible for our own actions and choices. Not the prince."

The girl smiled then at Struan and nodded. Clearly his words had been what she'd wanted to hear. But the smile left her face when Soni faced Fee.

"There must be a sacrifice made to earn his life," Soni said.

"I will pay the cost."

"Fiona, nay!" he shouted at her as he strode to her side. "Soni, the lass doesna understand the way of things with yer powers." He took her by the shoulders and gave her a gentle shake. "Do not do this, Fiona. Ye have given up so much."

"I accept," Soni said. She raised her hands and the green glow became so bright it was painful. It spread out from the girl and surrounded her, eating up the air and ground between them. Fee raised a hand to shield her eyes from it.

"Soni, I beg ye," Struan shouted.

His words had no affect on the girl's actions, for her power burst forth so strongly that even Fee could feel it. She was tempted to back away but Struan grabbed her.

Be happy, Struan. Do not stop telling yer stories.

Fee did not hear the words, but they echoed through her thoughts in the girl's voice. Staring into the green, she tried to find Soni.

Fear not, Fiona Masters. Ye have but to sacrifice yer guilt to keep him. Love will heal yer wounds and his.

The winds rose and swirled about the girl and then, an instant later, she was gone. Fee stood there, trying to comprehend what had just happened. The expression on Struan's face told her that he was just as shocked as she was.

"Why did ye do that? What did she ask of ye, lass?" he asked.

"You didn't hear her?" He shook his head. "She said I had to give up my guilt." She left out the rest, that was something for another day.

"Can ye do that, Fiona? Are ye ready?"

"I can if you will, Struan."

For a moment, they stood there as the possibilities spread out before them. Fee could begin to feel hope unfurl within her heart, hope for him, for her, for them. Hope for all that could be.

"I am ready, lass."

For the first time in three years, two months, one week and four days, Fee looked forward to life. To what would happen the next day and the next and the next.

"I am, too, Struan," she said, holding out her hand.

He took hold of hers and, in that instant, Fee felt like he would never let her go. And she was fine with that.

EPILOGUE

September 2018
Culloden Battlefield
Drummossie Moor, Scotland

Struan didn't want to stop in the Visitors' Center, so Fee followed him outside to the edge of the moor. Watching him as he approached the place where he'd spent two hundred sixty-nine years, six months and twenty-three days of purgatory, she was struck by his enthusiasm and anticipation. This trip had taken almost three more years to make happen and now she found herself holding her breath as they took one step and another toward the area where the battle occurred.

"Am I walking too quickly, lass?" he asked,

stopping there and looking at her.

"No, Struan, I can keep up with you."

It was true … she could.

Once she'd decided to live, and with his love and help and support, Fee had improved physically and mentally. They'd found doctors and therapists and counselors and all sorts of treatments that had indeed worked to improve her overall health and her endurance and relieve her pain.

But, in spite of her improvement, he waited and took her hand and walked at her pace up the hill on the small paved path that led onto the battlefield. Fee noticed that he looked around and listened as they made their way, passing other tourists who snapped photos as they listened to their audio tour guides.

Struan had no interest in any of that.

"Do you feel anything, Struan?" she asked. They'd discussed this so many times—about what to expect and what he might hear or see—but now that they were there, in the place of his death, she was as nervous as he seemed to be.

"Nothing. Not a wisp of movement or sound."

"You said they might be gone by now? If Soni was sending everyone off, they might not be here." His expression fell then as he took in the reality that they might be. "Wait. Where did you all gather? What spot here is where she called you all together?"

"Up on the field, near where the cairn is," he said,

nodding across the moor to the stone monument. "Can ye—"

"Yes, Struan. I can."

This time, she had to concentrate on walking because he did walk faster. She couldn't blame him, though. They reached the tall, stone cairn marking the center of the battlefield.

"'Twas different then. Over the centuries, so many changes occurred. I canna remember when this was placed here, but they marked the graves along that path then, too. Well, they guessed about many of them."

"Tell me of the battle, Struan." He released her hand and took a few paces away. "If you would?"

"Aye, lass," he said as he turned around, trying to get his bearings. "It looks so different to me now. For so long, it all appeared in shades of grey and mist. Now, to see the heather and the gorse on the moor and the sunshine as it moves across the fields, it is so different."

He guided her to a small bench there on the side of the path and then pointed off in the distance to a row of flags. She'd gone online and studied up on all the information she could find about the battle and the field and yet, as he started to tell it, she remembered none of it.

"The government forces lined up where the red flags are and the Jacobites over there where the blue one lie."

His voice grew stronger as he told her about marching the night before in an attempt at a sneak attack on Cumberland's forces nearer to Nairn. She found herself drawn into the story, though this one was not a tale, but true and far more precise than even the ones told by the trained guides or docents here. It was not that they didn't try to be accurate—they did. But he had lived and died it and knew details of the attempts to place the Stuarts back on the throne that modern-day historians could only dream about.

It was not long before others gathered around them, listening to him tell the story of that fateful battle and the men who'd fought in it. And yet, each word he spoke seemed to only be for her. His gaze moved from hers out to the fields and flags and the roads nearby and the cottage and back to her, never realizing that others, strangers, listened, too.

She lost track of time and simply focused on his voice. One of the things she enjoyed most about their time together was the nights when he would read aloud to her. It was those hours that led her to suggest he should narrate audiobooks. Struan had thought her mad, especially when she told him about the thousands of books that had been converted to recordings. And how a deep, Scottish-accented voice like his could be very popular.

He'd laughed then and he laughed when he was offered his first book to read. Now, he continued to do it when their schedule allowed him the time for it.

The polite applause broke into her reverie and she watched as he blushed at their response. Unaware of his audience during the whole of his tale, Struan nodded and thanked them. More than a few of those watching approached him with questions and it was some time before they were alone there once more.

"So, that was the whole of it then?" she asked, standing when he reached out to her. He gathered her close, with his arm around her shoulders, and they stood in the chilly morning air together.

"Aye, the whole thing told in order and told the way it all happened."

"Do you think any of them heard it? Do you think they know what happened to you?"

"Nay, lass. I think them all gone by now."

She turned into his embrace and reached up to his face. "I am sorry that we could not get here sooner. I wish we'd been here in time."

"I do as well, Fiona."

Even the vast amount of money and assets she held in the companies her parents had built were not enough to sort through the legal matters that happened when a previously non-existent person needed all the papers and documents to prove their identity and origin. It had taken until just two months ago to provide him with a British passport and birth certificate so he could travel outside the US and so that they could marry… legally. And the process of procuring those documents had not been accomplished easily… and maybe not have even been completely within legal bounds. But, her money did smooth over much of that.

He let out a slow breath then. "I kenned that Soni had a plan. Even for someone as young as she, she seemed to follow a pattern in what she did."

"And you have no idea where she is from or where she lives?"

"Nay. I fear not."

"And now?"

"I would like to walk a bit," he said, glancing out over the moor that had been his prison for so long. "Will ye join me?"

"You go on. I will head back to the Visitors' Center and wait for you there."

She gave no excuse for that, for she understood what he needed. His green eyes glimmered with unshed tears as he nodded and walked off. He needed to be alone there. He needed his chance to say farewell to this hallowed place before he could truly move on.

So, Fee made her way down the path, taking her time and not looking back at him. He would find his way to her when he was ready. She'd nearly reached the entrance to the center when he grabbed her from behind and kissed her neck.

"Thank ye for that. I love ye, lass."

"I love you, Storyteller. Are you ready to go?"

"It will take us about two hours of driving to reach Achnacarry," he whispered in her ear. "If we drive along Loch Ness, ye might see the monster that lives there."

"Is that another story of yours?"

"Nay, not mine, but I amna above using someone else's good story when I need to, lass."

Fee laughed then as they made their way to the rented car and began the next part of their journey south to the Cameron Clan lands where he'd been born. As he spoke yet again of his grandmother's penchant for marrying a number of men and shooting her husbands as they irritated her, Fee prayed that he would be able to tell tales of their lives soon.

And even if they all began with the story of how she shot him the first moment they met, she knew that their story would end in happily-ever-after.

Please Enjoy this excerpt from

A Traitor's Heart

from BRANDYWINE BRIDES:
A Blackwood Legacy Anthology

1721

Finlan Blackwood has survived fighting on the losing side of the Jacobite Rising, but finds himself transported to Pennsylvania in the Colonies to serve out his sentence for treason. Five years and he'll be free to seek out his family in the south and to regain his life. But when the widow Elizabeth Graham find herself at the mercy of an unscrupulous nobleman, Finn must decide if he should follow his family or follow his traitorous heart.

Prologue

Philadelphia, Pennsylvania
July, 1716

Fin shielded his eyes against the midday, midsummer sun and stared out over the gathered crowd. Some there, he noticed, stared back at him, openly inspecting and evaluating him much like a piece of horseflesh or beast of burden.

Which, in truth, he now was.

He shuffled along the raised platform, until the line of men before and after him stopped. They were called forward one at a time and each man called out his name and occupation. When the man in charge pointed at him, Fin took a step forward as he fought the urge to run and the need for sustenance. His knees shook when he moved too quickly and his voice quivered like a wee bairn when he could speak.

"Finlan Blackwood," he said. The words came out

as a squeak so he swallowed hard against the dryness of his mouth and spoke louder this time. "Finlan Blackwood."

"What skills have you?" the man asked. "Were you trained for an occupation, boy?"

'Twas a hard thing, to concentrate on what the man said, with all the people staring and the sun beating down on him. He'd never gone this long eating and drinking so little. Even the months in the prison before his transportation had not been as terrible as the journey on this ship across the Atlantic Ocean to this hot, humid place.

"Skills, boy?" the man yelled a bit louder and pushed at his shoulder with a wooden cudgel.

"My da is … was a blacksmith," he answered, sorrow and exhaustion filling his voice and tightening his throat. "He trained me." His father and the rest of his family were dead or gone now. The only kith or kin he had were scattered along the coastal colonies, transported for their crime of treason against the English Crown and sold, as he would be, into indenture.

"A blacksmith!" the man called out. "A man….–" he began. "A boy with skills and much potential to the right buyer!" The seller poked and prodded him again, but he met with flaccid skin and little muscle.

The man's words blurred as the next five years of his life were offered into bonded servitude. No matter the glowing words or points the man made, no one seemed interested. Then, when the man lowered the price, the cost of his transportation to the Colony plus the ship owner's fees, a tall man stepped forward. The man's garb and tall hat marked him a Quaker. A few minutes of quiet discussion led to Fin being directed down the steps and to a table. Sooner than he would have thought possible, he went from convict and traitor to bought-and-paid-for servant. An "X" marked the place on the contract where he had to sign his agreement to the terms.

Five years of good and hard work.

Food and a place to sleep.

His owner would set the rules.

Property now and no longer his own man.

His long-empty stomach clenched in bitter disagreement, but Fin forced his hand to mark the document. As a traitor and convict, Fin expected disrespect and loathing and was surprised to see something different in the Quaker's gaze.

"Come thou now," the man said quietly.

Before they took a step, Fin looked back at those yet remaining on the platform. Those men were the only links back to his homeland and his lost family. Some were distant cousins or neighbors who'd been caught up in the Jacobite uprising's fever. Some were prisoners with whom he'd shared a cell or, more lately, the hold of a ship.

"Have thou belongings to claim, Finlan?" the man asked.

Pain pierced him as surely as a dagger through his heart. The only thing he'd had was lost to him now. His mother had pressed her luckenbooth brooch into his hand as he'd left to follow his father into the fighting. The gemstones on it had saved his life several times but were gone now. Even the gnarled and bent metal had purchased some morsels of food in prison.

"Nay," he said, shaking his head. "I have only the clothes on my back."

The heavy hand on his shoulder spoke of a man used to the hard labor of working metal and yet his light touch gave Fin some succor.

"Thou hast thy life and thy soul and thy mind," the man said. "Many have begun a new life with less."

"A new life?" Fin had only thought on the deprivation and loss of the last year and not beyond it.

"Aye, Finlan Blackwood. Thou hast a new life, an open road before thee to makest what thou will of it. Most men never have this chance."

He stood a little taller then, for he had not considered this an opportunity. The others had spoken of the harshness ahead of them and not once had he thought of the possibilities. Five years was a long time, but if he worked hard for this man who seemed a fair one, he would earn his freedom. If he learned the trade his father had pointed him to, he would have a way to make a living. Then, he could seek out those kin he knew lived farther south, in the Carolinas and try to establish a life and family there. Just then, his life did not seem as filled with loss as it had been minutes ago.

"What do I call ye, sir?" he asked.

"Neither lord nor sir, nor any term that sets one above another," the man said. "Those in *Fellowship* use our given names to address others. My name is Richard Montgomery. So, thou may call me Richard or Friend Richard or simply Friend."

Fin held out his hand and took a firm grasp of the Quaker's larger one.

"Richard," Fin said, shaking his hand. "Friend."

"Come, let us see to getting thee some sustenance and then I can finish my errands here in town."

Fin's stomach grumbled loudly at just the mention of food. His ma had said he ate for three men. His ma … there would be time enough to mourn and grieve, but not now. Now, he had just been given a gift by this man. Questions flooded his thoughts then and he asked them as they walked away from the harbor.

"Where will I live?" he asked.

"Thou will live with me and mine," Richard replied. "My smithy is at the edge of the town, to the south." Richard pointed to the left and off in the distance. "And I offer my services out into Chester County, as well, where my farm lies," he added. "That is where thou will work whilst thou learn the craft better."

Fin followed the man and climbed into the wagon Friend Richard indicated was his when they reached it by the public house. They rode in silence through the busy town to its edge.

Five years.

In five years, his debt would be paid and Fin would be his own man, free to come and go as he pleased.

In five years, he would seek out his kin and make his life with them.

Five years.

Chapter One

Cooper's Farm, Chester County
July 1721

Taking her ease in the shadows created by the front porch, Elizabeth stood in silence and stared across the fields at the dust rising from the road to the east. The clouds above her and the humidity that thickened the air around her promised that the dust would soon be weighted down with moisture. Dust to mud with one afternoon shower was usual for this time of the year in this corner of southern Pennsylvania.

The sound of a cart's wooden wheels was familiar as they approached. The blacksmith was making his rounds of the farms along the Brandywine River, repairing the farming implements and preparing the metal scythes and plow blades for the coming harvest. As soon as the cart turned onto the lane leading to the house, Elizabeth realized it was not Friend Richard but his man, Finlan Blackwood. He nodded as he slowed the cart before her.

"Mistress Graham, how do ye fare this fine day?" he asked. A trace of the Highland accent yet flavored his voice even these five years since his arrival. Elizabeth tugged the handkerchief free from the wristband of her sleeve and mopped her brow.

"Is that what you call it, Mr. Blackwood?" she asked, smiling. Thunder rumbled above them, making one of her points.

"Just so, Mistress," he said, laughing.

Even a God-fearing widow like herself could not help but notice the deepness of his laugh and the broadness of his shoulders. Or the way his voice had deepened as he reached maturity. He'd grown up well these last five years since his arrival here. Aye, he'd grown up well.

"Is there something on my jacket?" Mr. Blackwood asked, brushing his hand over his shoulder as he spoke. He'd caught her staring. So much for the God-fearing and respectable widow demeanor for which she'd striven.

If truth be told, she had enjoyed the physical side of her marriage to Jonah and missed the closeness of it. Still, gawping at the blacksmith would not bring Jonah back or accomplish anything of what yet stood undone in her day. Such as finding a way to pay this man for repairs he would perform on the plows on her farm.

"Nay," she answered, glancing into the distance to cover her perusal. "I was just looking for Nathaniel in the southern field."

The blacksmith turned to look in that direction and the width of those wide, muscled shoulders now blocked her view of anything else. Aye, he had grown up well.

"His leg still bothering him then?" Now, he removed the wide-brimmed hat from his head and raked his fingers through his auburn hair. Standing taller, he tossed his hat in the wagon and took a step away from her. "Would you like me to bring him back in the wagon?"

"There's no need," she said. "The cart is there."

He faced her then, the full force of those forest green eyes on hers, and nodded. 'Twas time to bring her shame to light. No matter how much she'd rather not reveal the terrible state of the farm's situation and her potential loss, Elizabeth was pragmatic enough to know she had run out of time, excuses and money.

"Mr. Blackwood, would you like a cool drink of water? I just brought up a pitcher from the springhouse." She forced a smile on her face and reached for the door. The house was not much more comfortable in temperature, but being out of the sun might bring some relief. And, she would speak easier if he was sitting and not towering over her as he did now.

"With gratitude, Mistress Graham."

She lifted the latch and pushed the door open. Blessed by its position on the hillside, the house caught the best breezes as they moved through the vale toward the Brandywine River. His heavy boot steps followed her inside and, after he'd passed her, she motioned to the kitchen. Leaving the door open, she walked to the table near the window and reached for the stone pitcher and cups there.

"Here, let me," he said, reaching past her to lift the heavy vessel. He managed to stand at her back and reach the pitcher without touching her, his long, strong arms easily lifting the water.

She'd not heard his approach but she was grateful for his help. Elizabeth brought the cups and he filled each one before placing the pitcher on the table. They sat across the well-worn table and Elizabeth took a sip before speaking again.

"I am afraid you have come all this way for nothing, Finlan." There, that was a good way to begin.

"Do yer implements no' need sharping for the harvest?" he asked. Though his fingers still encircled the cup, he did not partake of the water.

Elizabeth pulled her dignity and wits tighter around her and smiled at him, bravely putting on an expression she hoped showed a calm she did not feel. This would be but the first of many such encounters and admissions, so she steeled herself against the shame and fear before meeting his gaze.

"I cannot pay for your services, Finlan. I'm afraid there is not enough coin or crop to cover the cost of them."

Elizabeth had looked down at his hands as she finished admitting her situation and watched as they clutched the cup tightly. Now, she attempted to raise her eyes once more, knowing she must accept the pity she would see, first from him and then from others, once her circumstances were known among her neighbors and friends.

A clear gaze, neither pitying nor judging, met hers. A flash of something else shone there, but Elizabeth could not decipher its meaning. She searched his expression for his opinion and found only an openness she did not expect.

"I ken, Mistress Graham."

The quiet words pierced her. How? How did he know the truth?

"Worry no' on the cost for now. Without the right tools, ye cannot clear yer fields. I could not, in good conscience, allow a friend to face that if I could help them."

In one of their conversations over the last several months, Finlan Blackwood had revealed that he'd kept to his own faith in spite of living with Richard Montgomery, a faithful Friend. With his words, though, he'd shown that some of their practices had, indeed, rubbed off on him during his years here.

Still … his words were very much like a Friend in Community would utter. When he reached out and touched her hand with his, she understood that the action was not.

"Mistress Graham, is there no one to whom ye can turn in this distress? A relative or one of yer late husband's family? A friend?" Then, before she could reply, he pulled his hand back and shook his head. "Forgive me for my intrusion into a private matter," he said as he stood.

"You knew?" she asked. A quick and slight nod gave her his answer. If he knew, then who else did? Elizabeth stood as well, gathering the cups and taking them to the sink. "Does everyone know?"

"'Tis no secret from yer neighbors and others."

The shopkeepers who'd allowed her to purchase on credit. The other workmen who waited still for payment. Her neighbors who noticed the fewer and fewer fieldworkers and more uncultivated fields than fields ready for seed. His quiet admissions shredded her pride.

"So, then, I think you will find that the Camerons have need of your services now," she said. She walked through the cabin to the front door, not able to look at him. "I am sorry you came out this way for nothing."

"Elizabeth," he said softly, standing before her as

she fought the tears of failure.

Elizabeth? The fact that he'd used her given name finally struck her and forced her to lift her head. Now, those green eyes looked at her in compassion. Something else glowed there but she could not identify it.

"I will tend to the farm plows and blades. We will speak of payment when ye are able to."

When she wanted to argue, he shook his head and crossed those strong arms over his chest. For an insane moment, she wished he would wrap his arms around her and hold her close until her fears eased. Before she could say another word, he nodded at her.

"My thanks for the water. I will see to things," he said.

He walked through the open door without another word or glance. Within a few moments, she heard the sound of his wagon making its way around the house and up the road to the barn near the southern fields.

Only then, as he was almost out of sight, did she give in to the growing despair and fear. Elizabeth walked to the table, sat down once more. Leaning her head down, she covered her face with her hands and let the tears flow.

Only when the sounds of a song being sung drifted through the open door did she lift her head. The faint Scottish lilt in the voice of the singer made her smile.

Finlan Blackwood could carry a tune.

Meet Terri Brisbin

Award-winning and ***USA Today*** best-selling author, **Terri Brisbin** is a mom, a wife, grandmom! and a dental hygienist from southern NJ. Terri writes all sorts of sexy, compelling historical romances including those set in the medieval Highlands of Scotland, during times when the Vikings ruled and warred and in the Regency ballrooms of London and Edinburgh. Since she likes a glimmer of Celtic magic and myths, she's written paranormal historicals, time travel romances as well as a fantasy series. More than 3 million copies of her 50+ romance novels and novellas have sold in more than 25 countries and 20 languages around the world.

Her current and upcoming historical and paranormal/fantasy romances will be published by Oliver Heber Books, Dragonblade Publishing and Harlequin Historicals.

Connect with Terri:
Facebook: @TerriBrisbin
Facebook Author Page: @TerriBrisbinAuthor
Instagram: @TerriBrisbin

TerriBrisbin.com

The Ghosts of Culloden Moor--by L.L. Muir unless noted otherwise

1. The Gathering
2. Lachlan
3. Jamie
4. Payton
5. Gareth (Diane Darcy)
6. Fraser
7. Rabby
8. Duncan (Jo Jones)
9. Aiden (Diane Darcy)
10. Macbeth
11. Adam (Cathie MacRae)
12. Dougal
13. Kennedy
14. Liam (Diane Darcy)
15. Gerard
16. Malcolm (Cathie MacRae)
18. Watson
19. Iain (Melissa Mayhue)
20. Connor
21. MacLeod (Cathie MacRae)
22. Murdoch (Diane Darcy)
23. Brodrick
24. The Bugler
25. Kenrick (Diane Darcy)
26. Patrick (Cathie MacRae)
27. Finlay
28. Hamish
29. Rory (Jo Jones)
30. MacBean (Diane Darcy)
31. Tristan
32. Niall (Diane Darcy)
33. Fergus (Bess McBride)
34. Angus (Jo Jones)
35. Bram
36. Alexander (Cassidy Cayman)
37. Ronan (Diane Darcy)
38. The Blacksmith
39. Ross (Jennae Vale)
40. Alistair (Jo Jones
41. MacNabb (Diane Darcy)
42. Rhys
43. Gregor (Jo Jones)
44. Jack
45. The Storyteller (Terri Brisbin)
46. Moodie
47. Chisholm (Jo Jones)
48. Dallas (Cassidy Cayman)
49. Fisher
50. The Reckoning
51. Wyndham
52. Calum (Diane Darcy)
53. McColl (Jo Jones)
54. Giver
55. Harry
56. Urban
57. Sean (Jo Jones)
58. Knox
59. Alice (Diane Darcy
60. A Wee Wager
61. St. Leger
62. MacTavish
63. Tulloch
64. The Thief
65. Sweeney (Diane Darcy)

66. McIsaac (Jo Jones)
67. Leif
68. O'Reilly (Diane Darcy)
69. The Dragon and the Watcher
70. The Time Traveler (Jo Jones)
71. Wallace
72. MacGillivray (Diane Darcy)
73. The Whisperer (Jennae Vale)
74. Cooper
75. A Touch of Magic (Diane Darcy)
76. The Guardian (Jo Jones)
77. Fenton (Cassidy Cayman)
78. The Last Highlander
79. The Wedding

Other Books by
by Terri Brisbin

A HIGHLAND FEUDING Series:
Stolen by the Highlander
The Highlander's Runaway Bride
Kidnapped by the Highland Rogue
Claiming His Highland Bride
A Healer for the Highlander
The Highlander's Inconvenient Bride – crossover with the CLAN MACLERIE series
Her Highlander for One Night

UNEXPECTED HEIRS OF SCOTLAND series:
The Lady Takes It All
A Lady's Agreement

The MACKENDIMEN CLAN Series:
A Love Through Time
Once Forbidden
A Highlander's Hope (novella)
A Matter of Time

WARRIORS OF THE STONE CIRCLES Series:
Rising Fire
Raging Sea
Blazing Earth

The STORM Series:
A Storm of Passion
A Storm of Love novella
A Storm of Pleasure
Mistress of the Storm

The CLAN MACLERIE Series:
Taming the Highlander
Surrender to the Highlander
Possessed by the Highlander
Taming The Highland Rogue
The Highlander's Stolen Touch
At The Highlander's Mercy

The Forbidden Highlander in HIGHLANDERS
The Highlander's Dangerous Temptation
Yield to The Highlander
The Highlander's Inconvenient Bride – crossover with A Highland Feuding series!
Her Highlander for One Night

Related stories (same clan 500 years later)
The Earl's Secret
Blame It On The Mistletoe in ONE CANDLELIT CHRISTMAS

The DUMONT Series:
The Dumont Bride
The Norman's Bride
The Countess Bride
Love at First Step from THE CHRISTMAS VISIT
The King's Mistress
The Claiming of Lady Joanna from THE BETROTHAL

The KNIGHTS of BRITTANY Series:
A Night for Her Pleasure
The Conqueror's Lady
The Mercenary's Bride
His Enemy's Daughter

STAND-ALONE STORIES:
The Queen's Man
The Duchess's Next Husband
The Maid of Lorne
Kidnapping the Laird
What The Duchess Wants – for newsletter subscribers only!
Upon A Misty Skye
Across A Windswept Isle
A Traitor's Heart in BRANDYWINE BRIDES
The Storyteller – A Ghosts of Culloden Moor Novella
An Outlaw's Honor ~ A Midsummer Knights romance
Tempted by Her Viking Enemy
The Highlander's Substitute Wife (HIGHLAND ALLIANCES series)

Made in the USA
Las Vegas, NV
21 August 2024